AS WHITE
AS SNOW

ALSO BY SALLA SIMUKKA

As Red As Blood

THURSDAY, 16 JUNE

1

I'm only happy when it rains.

Shirley Manson's voice flowed into Lumikki's ears, assuring her that she only listened to sad songs, only found comfort in black nights and always loved bad news. The sun shone in a perfectly cloudless sky. Eighty-two-degree heat sent sweat trickling down Lumikki's back. Her arms and legs were sticky. If she had licked the back of her hand, she would have tasted salt. Each strap on her sandals felt like one too many. Her toes and the soles of her feet yearned for freedom.

Sitting down on a stone wall, Lumikki took off her sandals, pulled up her legs and wiggled her toes. A group of Japanese tourists stared. A couple of the young women giggled. Hadn't they ever seen bare feet before? *Hello, I'm from the land of the Moomins. Moomins don't wear shoes.*

It wasn't raining. It hadn't rained for five days.

I'm only happy when it rains. Lumikki couldn't sing along with Shirley because then she would be lying. The sun was shining and she was happy. She didn't want things to be complicated. She didn't feel good only when things were going wrong. Shirley could keep her dark emotions. Lumikki switched off

3

the music and let the noise of the tourists take possession of her sound world.

Italian, Spanish, American English, German, French, Japanese, Russian . . . In the melee of languages, it was tough to pick out individual words, let alone phrases. Which was actually a relief, because then she didn't have to concentrate on the pointless repetition of obvious banalities. Lumikki knew exactly what most people said at this spot.

What a view!

And it was. There was no denying it. The view over Prague was stunning. Red-tile roofs, treetops, church towers, bridges, the Vltava River glittering in the sun. The city took Lumikki's breath away. Even after five days, she still wasn't used to this sight. Every day, she made her way to some high place just to gaze at the city and feel this inexplicable joy.

Maybe it was the freedom of detachment and solitude she felt. She was completely on her own. She wasn't accountable to anyone. No one was calling for her and no one wanted to know her schedule. She didn't have a single responsibility. Thoughts of preparing for her senior year of high school and working for the second half of the summer could wait until she was back in Finland. Now there was only her, the blazing heat and the city, which breathed deep sighs of history.

It was 16 June. Lumikki only had a week left of her Prague holiday before she was supposed to return to Finland to spend a traditional midsummer with her extended family, this year in the Turku archipelago. She hadn't known how to refuse when her father had assumed that of course Lumikki would come. She didn't have anything else going on, did

4

she? A cabin rented with some friends? Special plans with a special someone?

No, nothing. Lumikki would have preferred to spend midsummer at her apartment, alone, listening to the silence. She didn't yearn for merry schnapps songs, new potatoes or herring. She didn't want to play the role of the diligent schoolgirl, smiling and chatting politely, giving vague answers to questions about the future and boyfriends, pushing away uncles who weren't biologically related and hugged her just a little too tight.

But she understood that her dad really wanted her to come. And her mum too. Only three and a half months had passed since Lumikki had been lying in hospital. She'd been shot in the thigh, but luckily the bullet had only grazed the skin. The frostbite she'd got from lying in the snow had been worse. Trying to unravel the mystery of a rubbish bag full of bloodstained cash tossed into her schoolmate Elisa's backyard had got her in trouble with a gang of drug runners. Tracking Elisa's dad, a narcotics cop on the take, had led Lumikki to a lavish party at a carefully guarded mansion. There, she'd learned that the leader of the drug smuggling operation, known as Polar Bear, was actually two women who were identical twins. Lumikki had been forced to flee when Boris Sokolov, Polar Bear's thug, had recognised her.

Based on Lumikki's testimony, Sokolov and Elisa's father had both ended up behind bars, but no one could lay a finger on the Polar Bear twins. After everything that happened in March, Lumikki had decided that, from now on, she truly was never going to stick her nose in anyone else's business ever again. She had been chased, nearly frozen in a freezer, and shot. That was quite enough, thank you very much. No more blood. No more sleuthing or running for her life through the snow wearing slippery combat boots.

For a while, Lumikki's mum and dad had wanted to keep her at home in Riihimäki, north of Helsinki. They had even wanted to give notice on Lumikki's apartment in Tampere, but Lumikki wouldn't hear of it. She spent all spring delivering newspapers to cover the rent, convincing her parents to keep the apartment 'just in case'. For the first few weeks, though, there was no point trying to get them to let her stay there overnight. Lumikki just accepted the situation and took the train all the way to Tampere for school every day. Gradually, her parents saw how impractical the commute was, and Lumikki started slowly moving her things back into the apartment. One night there turned to two, two turned to three, and eventually, in May, she announced that she would only be dropping by their home in Riihimäki every once in a while. Full stop. Her parents didn't say anything. How could they have stopped her? She was practically an adult, after all. Lumikki could pay the rent from savings and the small student stipend she received if she had to.

After school had ended, Lumikki had wanted a break. She'd booked a ticket to Prague, looked for a suitably inexpensive room in a hostel, packed her backpack with just the bare necessities and left.

The moment the aeroplane took off, she could feel the relief in her gut. Time away from Finland. Away from her parents' constant anxiety. Away from the streets where she sometimes

6

still flinched when she saw a man dressed all in black. Lumikki had spent her whole life fighting fear. She hated fear. As she had walked off the plane at the Prague airport, she felt the heavy chains loosen their grip. Her posture straightened and her steps became surer.

That's why Lumikki was happy. That's why she turned her face towards the sun, closing her eyes and smiling to herself. Breathing in the scents of Central Europe. Digging through her backpack, she pulled out a postcard of the Charles Bridge lit up at night. She decided to write a few lines to Elisa, who was 'Jenna' now because she and her mother had changed their names. That was the only way for them to stay safe after what had happened in the winter with Elisa's father. Lumikki still thought of Elisa as Elisa, though.

They lived in Oulu now, in the north of Finland, and Elisa was studying cosmetology. She wrote to Lumikki from time to time to keep her up to date. In her last letter Elisa had written about finally visiting her father in prison and how it hadn't felt as bad as she had imagined it would. It had been important to see her dad. In her letters, Elisa sounded surprisingly calm and a little more mature than before. The events of the winter had forced her to grow up and take responsibility. She couldn't be daddy's little girl any more and, surprisingly, that seemed to fit her much better than her previous role. Lumikki was pleased that things were going so well for her, given the circumstances.

Actually, Elisa had made this trip possible. She'd sent Lumikki a thousand euros from the thirty thousand thrown into the yard before turning most of the rest over to the police.

Lumikki had told her parents that she had saved the money for the trip herself. She did have some savings, but Elisa's gift meant she hadn't needed to touch them. It felt good to get the blood money used up and out of the secret compartment in her dresser where it never seemed to leave her alone.

Suddenly, a shadow fell over her face. The scent of incense mingled with a hint of hemp soap overpowered the general smell of the city. Lumikki opened her eyes. Next to her stood a girl in her twenties wearing white linen trousers and a loose, long-sleeved shirt made of the same material. Her brown hair was done in two braids that wrapped around her head to form a crown. There was uncertainty in her grey eyes. The girl fingered the worn leather strap of her shoulder bag, which was the colour of cognac.

Lumikki felt mild irritation.

She had seen the girl a couple of times before. She'd been watching Lumikki, apparently thinking she wouldn't notice. They had happened to go to the same tourist spots and been out around town at the same time. The girl looked a couple of years older than Lumikki and was also on her own. Probably some sort of hippie looking for a travelling companion to sit around with in parks, drinking warm, cheap red wine and discussing the deep interconnectedness of the universe.

Not that there was anything wrong with that, but Lumikki had come to Prague specifically to be alone. She didn't want any new friends.

When the girl opened her mouth, Lumikki had already planned what she would say. It would be brief, polite and cold. Cold always worked.

Despite the hot weather, though, by the time the girl reached the end of her sentence, a different kind of cold had crept up Lumikki's spine and made the hairs on her neck stand on end.

'Jag tror att jag är din syster.'

I think I'm your sister.

I am your blood. I am your flesh. You are my blood. You are my flesh.

We are one family. We are mothers and fathers, parents and children, sisters and brothers, aunts and uncles and cousins. Through us flows the same blood and the same faith, which is stronger than the mountains and deeper than the seas. God created us as one family, members of the same holy congregation.

Let us take each other by the hand. Sisters and brothers, our time will soon come. Jesus is calling us, and we will not hesitate to heed his call. We do not fear. Our faith is strong.

Our faith is as white as snow. It is pure and bright. It leaves no room for doubt. Our faith is like the light that will blind the sinners with its strength. Our faith will burn them even as the stubble of the field is devoured by fire.

We are the family that will always be one. We are the Holy White Family, and our patience will soon receive its reward.

2

The girl's eyes scanned the café tables, the patio umbrellas, the faces of the tourists. Her slender, white fingers stroked the surface of her glass of iced water, drawing lines in the moisture condensing on it. She had only taken one sip, while Lumikki had already downed two large glasses of water along with her small cup of black coffee.

They had settled on the overpriced tourist café in the courtyard of the castle because there wasn't anywhere else decent in the area. Lumikki's mind was tripping in circles. She didn't know how to formulate the dozens of questions jostling for attention in her head.

'*Jag måste kanske försöka förklara . . .*' the girl said uncertainly, barely above a whisper.

Yes, please do explain.

Lumikki stayed silent, deciding to let the girl tell her own story. No leading questions.

'*Jag har . . . kan jag prata engelska? Min svenska är lite . . . dålig.*'

By all means, speak English, Lumikki thought as she nodded. She noticed that the girl spoke with a strong Czech accent. Swedish was not her native language. There had to be a reason she had addressed Lumikki in Swedish instead of Czech or English, though.

'My name is Lenka. I'm twenty years old,' she said.

Lumikki looked at her fingers, which continued their nervous movements on the surface of the water glass. On her left hand, a faint depression was just visible running around her ring finger, as if she had worn a ring for a long time and only recently taken it off.

Lenka said that she had lived her whole life in Prague. She'd lived with her mother until the woman died when Lenka was fifteen. In an accident. A fall into the river at night.

Lenka's voice grew thick. For a few long moments, she stared over the tourists' heads towards the church, then eventually resumed her story.

'Since then . . . other people have taken care of me. Now I have a new family.'

'Are you married?' Lumikki asked.

Lenka shook her head violently.

'No, no, nothing like that. They are just good people who took me in. Do you believe in goodness?'

The question came so suddenly and with such earnestness that Lumikki had to take a sip of coffee before answering.

'I believe in good deeds. And good intentions.'

Lenka looked her straight in the eyes. Lumikki didn't know how to interpret her expression. Was it contemplative or belligerent? She wished Lenka would get to the point, but refrained from rushing her.

As if she'd read Lumikki's mind, Lenka said, 'When I was small, my mother wouldn't tell me anything about my father, even

14

though my pestering must have driven her crazy. "You don't have a father," was all she would say. I knew that was a lie. Everyone has a father. When I turned ten, my mother sat me down. Eleven years earlier, during the summer, she'd met a tourist. He was from Finland and spoke Swedish. His name was Peter Andersson.'

Lumikki felt cold again, even though the sweltering air pressed down on them from every side like an electric blanket. Automatically, she started searching Lenka's face for her father's features. Was there something similar in her straight, narrow nose? Her dark eyebrows? The shape of her jaw? At moments, she could almost see her father's face flickering in front of Lenka's, but then the vision would disappear.

'According to my mother, the relationship was brief and intense. The man had a wife in Finland. I was a mistake, of course, but when my mother discovered she was pregnant, she decided to keep me. She didn't tell the man – I mean, my father – anything at that point. It wasn't until I was two that she sent him a picture of me.'

Lenka paused for a moment and took a greedy gulp of water. Lumikki felt as if her chair were rocking under her. She was hearing Lenka's words, but having a hard time processing them. Her father had another daughter. Here. Her older sister.

'My father wanted to meet me, but Mother refused. For years, he sent letters, cards, pictures, little gifts and money for us. She never replied in any way and so, eventually, the letters became less frequent. Finally, they stopped altogether. Mother told me about my father, but not about the letters. I found them myself when I was twelve. Mother had hidden them in a box in the closet behind some sheets. I only had a few

15

minutes to look through everything before Mother walked in and flew into a rage. She accused me of snooping behind her back. She grabbed the box and emptied the contents into the stove, burning everything up. I spent the whole night crying.'

Lenka spoke in a dull, reedy voice, but the trembling of her hands betrayed that saying these words wasn't easy for her. For a long time, she sat silently, clearly not knowing how to continue.

Next to them was a boisterous group of Italian schoolchildren. The boys were chugging Cokes, competing to see who could burp the loudest. An American couple complained loudly about how confusing it was trying to convert euros to dollars and figure out whether they were really getting a bargain. Lumikki registered all of this, but the sounds felt as though they were coming from somewhere far away, from another dimension.

Lenka's story was like a puzzle piece falling into place and filling a hole Lumikki had felt as long as she could remember. She had always known, sensing that her family was hiding something. There was something big that no one would talk about but that sometimes filled the rooms of their house so densely it was hard to breathe. Her father's tenseness. Her mother's sad, tearful eyes. The conversations that cut off abruptly when Lumikki entered a room.

But still, Lumikki had a hard time imagining anything like this about her father. Peter Andersson was such a restrained man, so controlled and beyond reproach. A lot of people had a public face and a private face. At home, they could show the sorrow and exhaustion and regret they really felt. With their families, they could laugh and relax. Lumikki had always felt like her father only had a public face. He was always the same, wherever he was. The shell around him was strong and thick.

Could her father have had a torrid liaison in Prague? Was her father even capable of that kind of passion? He'd never said a word about visiting the city. It was strange. You'd have thought he would have given her tips about where to visit and what sights not to miss.

Lenka was talking about a Peter Andersson who Lumikki didn't recognise. That didn't mean anything, though. It was entirely possible that there were sides to her father Lumikki didn't know. Do we ever really know anyone else? Even the people closest to us?

'When Mother died, I thought I would never learn anything more about my father. All I had was a name, Peter Andersson, and the fact that he lived in Finland and spoke Swedish. The name was so common it didn't help at all. Then I saw you.'

'But how did you know?' Lumikki couldn't help asking. 'We've never met.'

For the first time, a small smile appeared on Lenka's lips.

'Before Mother burned the letters and everything, I saw a photograph of you. You were eight years old. On the back of the picture it said, *'Din lillasyster Lumikki.'* Your little sister Lumikki. That picture was seared on my mind, down to the smallest detail. When I saw you, I recognised you immediately. You look so much like your picture. But I wanted to be sure, so I followed you and watched. I hope you aren't angry.'

Lumikki shook her head. As she did so, she realised she wasn't entirely sure what she was saying no to.

All she knew was that nothing would ever be the same again.

3

Her hair was brown, like Lumikki's, but tending more towards mousey than warm auburn. And it was long. If she had undone her braided crown, Lenka's hair probably would have reached the small of her back. Lumikki's short bob was modelled after Carey Mulligan's. You couldn't tell anything from hair colour, though. Brown hair like theirs was probably the most common natural colour for women in Central Europe.

Grey eyes. Lenka's were a little darker than Lumikki's. Maybe the curve of her upper lip had the same softness, if you looked closely. The proportions of her face were different, though. Lenka's forehead was noticeably higher, and Lumikki's nose was shorter and smaller.

They were about the same height. Lenka was maybe an inch taller. Standing side by side in front of the café restroom's mirror, they inspected each other's faces. Lenka held Lumikki by the shoulder, which made Lumikki uncomfortable. She didn't like strangers touching her. Even with people she knew, she preferred to maintain her personal space. There were only a few people she let close enough to touch her. Lenka's grip was strong. Her face was just as white as her fingers. Lumikki had a light tan.

In terms of their outward appearance, they could have been sisters. Or not. No one single feature advertised a genetic relationship. And neither of them looked particularly like Lumikki's father.

Lumikki leaned over the sink and splashed her face and neck with cold water. That refreshed her and got her brain moving better. The action also made Lenka let go of her.

'What do you think?' Lenka asked, looking at Lumikki with eager expectation. Like a little puppy begging to be scratched behind the ear. Lumikki would have preferred not to say anything. Too much to process for one day. Too many revelations. She hadn't had time to think about what this would mean. What she would do.

Lumikki couldn't stand not knowing what she should do next.

'This is . . . an awful lot all at once,' she finally said, wiping her neck with a paper towel. One trickle of water had managed to slip under her shirt collar and now it ran down her spine like a dark premonition.

'I know. I've had years to work through this. You just heard it.'

'Yeah. Dad never said anything. I didn't know you existed. Dad . . .'

Now Lenka placed her other hand on Lumikki's shoulder. Apparently, she interpreted the hesitation as a surge of emotion. There was that, yes, but also the fact that, at this stage, Lumikki didn't want to reveal too much about herself. She had to make sure she knew the truth first.

There was something suspicious and agitated about Lenka and her story. The coincidences felt too big to be true. And yet, the details did seem to line up. Lumikki's thoughts were bouncing around wildly and she couldn't get them to settle.

'Can I ask you one favour? Don't tell your father about this yet. Our father. I don't want him to find out about me again through someone else. I want to tell him myself when the time is right,' Lenka said.

Lumikki nodded. It was any easy request to honour. Frankly, she hadn't even considered that her first order of business might be jumping on the phone and calling her dad to interrogate him about whether he had a secret daughter in Prague. That just wasn't what they did in their family. What they did was beat around the bush and try to settle things any way other than by talking openly. A family of secrets. Maybe that sounded exciting, like something from a mystery novel, but in reality it was like a huge boulder that weighed on all of them and made it hard to look each other in the eye.

'How did you learn Swedish?' Lumikki asked, switching languages.

Lenka smiled shyly and replied, also in Swedish. 'This probably sounds stupid, but when I learned that my father spoke Swedish, I started studying it on my own, using the internet and books. I watched clips of Swedish kids' shows on YouTube and tried to repeat the words. They felt strangely familiar in my mouth. *Smultron. Fånig. Längtan. Pannkaka.* Maybe our parents' languages are in our genes somehow.'

Lumikki didn't bother remarking on how that sounded like New Age gibberish, clearly lacking any grounding whatsoever in the science of genetics or human developmental psychology. Lenka could believe whatever she wanted.

A German tourist came into the women's restroom and gave Lumikki and Lenka a strange look. From outside came the sound of the bells from Saint Vitus Cathedral. Two o'clock in the afternoon. Lenka froze.

'Is it two already?' she asked.

Lumikki nodded. Lenka's gaze started darting around and her fingers went to the strap of her leather bag again. She looked like a hunted animal. The warmth and even slight relaxation in her bearing vanished in an instant.

'I have to go,' Lenka said. 'Let's meet tomorrow. At twelve.'

'Same place?'

Lenka glanced around.

'No. Not here. That's not a good idea. Do you know Vyšehrad, the fort? You can get there on the metro. Let's meet there.'

Lumikki didn't have time to say anything, not to suggest a more convenient meeting place or ask where Lenka was rushing off to, since she'd already dashed out of the restroom, leaving Lumikki frowning at herself in the mirror.

The woman's fingers drummed on the tabletop. The table felt slick. Just a month earlier, it had been sanded and lacquered, removing all the little scuffs. Her eyes scanned the walls of the room. There they were. The diplomas, the awards, the newspaper clippings, a colourful display of her career highlights. It was enough to make anyone jealous. But for her, it wasn't enough. Nothing was. She couldn't let anything be enough. Not in this field. In this field, you had to stay hungry. You always had to want something bigger, better, more startling, more sensational, more moving, more

21

infuriating, more heartwarming. You needed novelty like you needed oxygen. You had to keep your finger on the pulse of the times. Or stay ahead of the times, if you could, and strike when people least expected it.

You had to be a topic of conversation. On everyone's lips. Here. Now. Tomorrow.

The woman grabbed a phone, opening it, removing its SIM card and swapping in a different one.

She rebooted the phone and selected a number no one could ever know she'd called. A man's voice answered on the first ring.

'Is he ready?' the man wanted to know.

'Not yet.'

'Remember that he can't know too much.'

'Of course I remember. I've been doing this long enough to understand the rules. He has to know as little as possible. Then his reactions will be authentic. That authenticity is what we need. We need real emotions.'

'And you understand the danger he'll be in? He might get hurt. He might even die.'

'We have to take that risk. And when all is said and done, martyrdom wouldn't be the worst scenario. I can think of at least one time a martyr's death gave a story legs.'

Laughter.

'You shouldn't say things like that to me. I might take offence.'

'I'm counting on your black sense of humour.'

'There isn't anything black in me but my humour. So everything is proceeding according to plan?'

'Yes.'

'Good. I have to hang up now. God bless.'

The woman hung up, smiling to herself.

She didn't need God's blessings now. Other people might though.

People are hungry for heroes. They want to see and hear and read how good always conquers evil. David and Goliath, Jesus and Satan, little hobbits and the mighty Sauron. They want to experience the hero overpowering the invincible, beating the unbeatable, slaying the immortal. They hunger for stories where the impossible becomes possible through the intervention of a fearless hero full of righteousness.

The hero has to be sympathetic and approachable. He has to be simultaneously close to the people and slightly above them. He can't be overwhelmingly superior. He has to fight and struggle. He has to experience hardship and pain. He has to be nearly destroyed so he can rise up even stronger for the final battle. A hero also has to be vulnerable. He has to have places the opposing force can strike at.

Just as important as the hero, perhaps even more important for the story, is his opponent. Evil. Powerful, enigmatic, cruel – the kind of evil that sends a chill down your spine. That kind of evil draws people's attention like a magnet. They want to deny the existence of evil, but it also fascinates them.

They devour the evil until they feel sick. Then they want someone to come and take the sickness away. They want a hero.

A successful hero story doesn't come without collateral damage. People have to die so the ones who get saved seem that much more precious.

Only death can make a legend.

FRIDAY, 17 JUNE, EARLY MORNING

4

There was a hole in the ceiling. It stared at Lumikki like a black, sightless eye. She stared back. She was wide awake.

The yellow light of the streetlamps penetrated the thin curtains of the hostel room windows. A dog barked in a nearby park. It was two o'clock in the morning. The oppressive heat of the day didn't seem to let up even at night, and Lumikki's sheets were soaked with sweat. She got up to open the window. She had to pull hard before the swollen frame gave way and the window opened with a rattle. The humid night air poured into the room, accompanied by the steady drone of traffic punctuated with car horns and squealing brakes. Someone accelerated with screeching tyres. A group of revellers returning from a bar began to sing. The only thing she could make out from their discordant voices was that they were probably singing in French.

Lumikki leaned on the windowsill. Even though the air outside was just as warm as inside, the light breeze dried the sweat on her skin. She wanted to take a shower, but that would be pointless because she'd just have to do it again in the morning. And Lumikki didn't feel like waking up half the hostel by setting off the clanking water pipes. She considered for a moment whether she might be hungry, but quickly rejected the idea of food. All she had were yesterday morning's pastries, which came in different shapes and looked delicious, but always turned out to be the same puff pastry with slightly variable fillings. Some were sweet and some savoury, but all of them left a greasy film on the roof of her mouth.

Either the heat or her nightmare must have woken her up. Or maybe both. The clammy sheets chafing against her skin might have triggered the nightmare. It was a familiar one, but she hadn't had it in years. After she started school, dreams about bullies had replaced it, nightmares that continued after the sun came up, repeating again and again until reality and dream intermingled, leaving her unable to say when she was awake and when she was asleep.

This nightmare was from earlier, though. From the years before she learned fear.

In the dream, Lumikki stood before a large mirror. She was little, about two years old. At first, all she could see in the mirror was herself and the dark room she was standing in. She lifted her arm and her mirror image did the same. She smiled. She grinned. The reflection did the same. Then, in the mirror, she saw another girl appear behind her in the room. The girl was a little older than her, but very similar in appearance. They were even wearing the same white dress.

The girl placed her hands on Lumikki's shoulder. The hands felt warm and safe. Then the girl leaned in and whispered '*Du är min syster alltid och alltid och alltid.*' You will be my sister for ever and ever and ever.

Lumikki turned to her.

Why the hell did she always turn, when she knew that nothing good would come of it? Up to that point in the dream, she felt fine. She felt warm. Then came the cold. No one was standing behind her. She was in the dark room all alone. She turned to look at the mirror again. The girl was there. She stroked Lumikki's hair and Lumikki felt her gentle touch. Lumikki wanted to slap the hand away, but when she tried, her hands met only air.

'*Vill du inte leka med mig?*' the girl in the mirror asked sadly. Don't you want to play with me?

Lumikki shook her head violently. She just wanted the girl to disappear. The girl wasn't real and Lumikki was afraid.

'*Jag blir så ledsen,*' the girl said. It makes me so sad.

Then she started to cry. Lumikki wanted to look away. She wanted to squeeze her eyes shut. But she couldn't help looking. Even though she knew. She knew she didn't want to see the girl's tears.

The tears were red. They were huge drops of blood that ran down the girl's cheeks and dripped from her chin, staining her dress with streaks of red. When Lumikki finally tore her gaze away, she looked down and saw that her own dress was no longer white. It, too, was covered in streaks of blood.

Then she woke up. Always at the same place.

Lumikki had never understood where the nightmare came from. Had she caught a glimpse of a scary movie by accident when she was little? Had one of the older children at daycare or the playground told her a ghost story?

It was obvious why the nightmare had returned now, though. You didn't have to be a dream analyst to figure that out. The

31

reflection of Lumikki and Lenka. Lenka's claim that they shared a father. That they were sisters. The parallels screamed so loudly she would have had to press her hands to her ears not to hear them. What made Lumikki shudder wasn't that the nightmare had returned after so many years. What gave her chills was that the dream might not be just a dream.

That didn't make any sense, though. If Lenka's story was true – which Lumikki wasn't ready to swallow, at least not yet – they'd never met before. So preschool-aged Lumikki couldn't have had a memory of standing in front of a mirror with her sister.

She didn't believe in visions. That was nonsensical drivel.

So this had to be just a coincidence. Or maybe she'd overheard something. Maybe a word here and a word there from her parents' otherwise carefully masked arguments had been enough to construct a tenuous image that twisted and expanded in her young mind into this nightmare. That sounded like the most plausible explanation.

Lumikki took in the night air with slow, deep breaths. The nightmare's grip loosened. Prague at night smelled of hope and broken promises. It smelled of history and dusty streets. It smelled sweet and savoury all at once.

Lumikki decided to leave the window open and try to sleep, despite the traffic and the sounds of the night. As she stepped back from the window towards the bed, fists suddenly began pounding on her door with such force that for a moment she thought it would come off its hinges.

Snatching the sheet from the bed, Lumikki wrapped it around her naked body. Then she grabbed the nearest thing that could serve as a weapon to protect herself. It was a half-empty water bottle. Her defences left something to be desired. Every muscle tense, she stared at the door. If the intruder got the door open, she would be ready to kick it back in his face. The inward-opening door would work in her favour. The element of surprise even more.

Lumikki stayed perfectly silent. That she knew how to do. She was a master at that.

The fists trying to pound through the door came again, this time even harder.

Lumikki hoped that a well-aimed blow with the water bottle could work too. First the door, then the bottle. That was her detailed plan of attack.

Just then, from outside the door came sounds of drunken laughter and attempts at singing.

'We like to party, party! We like to party, party! Come on, man! This is no time for sleep!'

Lumikki's shoulders relaxed. She let her hand holding the bottle fall. She realised before one of them did.

'Oh shit! We got the wrong room. It's 208, not 206.' As the merrymakers moved along to pound on the next door and repeat their chant, Lumikki crawled back into bed. Surprisingly, the cacophony coming from outside and in the hall made her eyelids droop shut immediately as a deep, dreamless sleep took her.

The man was awake. He was often awake in the small hours of the morning when everyone else in the house was asleep. A shepherd guarding his flock. That's what they thought, anyway, and they weren't completely wrong. They were his flock and he had been raising and shepherding them for years, more than twenty now. He had been patient and long-suffering. The man had told himself many times that if he could just wait long enough, he would be rewarded.

The man walked from room to room with soft, soundless steps. The rooms smelled a little dusty and stuffy, and they were full of the breath and dreams of sleeping people. He looked at the peaceful, slumbering faces. One mouth hung open a little, another clutched a pillow like a long-lost lover. They all looked small and fragile, even the men. They were like butterflies he could reach out and touch. He had the power to crush them, to pierce them with pins and make them part of his collection, to pluck their wings, to choke them with smoke or take away their oxygen.

He held their lives in his hands.

FRIDAY, 17 JUNE

5

Jiři Hašek squeezed two oranges into a glass and threw the juice back in a single gulp. The fresh, sweet flavour spread through his mouth, and he could almost feel the vitamins being absorbed into his bloodstream and giving him his morning pick-me-up. Looking out of the window at the city waking up to its morning bustle, he could tell the day would be sweltering again. A thin, misty layer of cirrus clouds covered the sky, but it curbed the blazing sun about as much as a veil cools the ardour of a bride gazing at her groom.

Jiři smiled to himself, thinking how he would look to an outsider, sitting in his penthouse apartment drinking freshly squeezed orange juice. Handsome, with his classically styled dark coiffure, straight-legged trousers and white collared shirt, he was like something out of an advertisement. The embodiment of success and vitality.

Jiři almost laughed out loud. He was only twenty-five years old. He had the job of his dreams. Every sign pointed to a career with a steep upward trajectory. He was an investigative TV journalist who could easily become the next big star in his field. He could have his own programme before he was thirty. He wasn't in a serious relationship, but that wasn't due to a lack of options, just a matter of personal choice. Jiři didn't want to make any serious commitments yet. He wanted to be able to flirt, to have adventures, to enjoy all the variety the world had to offer. He could settle down in a few years once he found a woman who was interesting and exciting enough.

Jiři Hašek was living his dream to its fullest and shamelessly loving every minute of it. He wasn't completely sure whether he deserved his position or this life, but he wasn't about to start apologising for it.

The youngest of a string of five siblings, Jiři had learned to stick up for himself and to grab some candy whenever it passed by. He was never the brightest student, but he was hungry for knowledge and had a knack for finding exactly the information that would help him get ahead. Sometimes that information was helpful to him and harmful to others. When Jiři discovered the relationship between his history teacher and the maths substitute – something he had caught hints of and then established definitively when he opened the copy room door at just the wrong moment for them and just the right moment for him – he didn't hesitate for a second. He demanded higher grades in history and maths, and, of course, received both.

The right information opened doors that would otherwise stay closed. Very early on Jiři realised that he had a nose for news and quickly found his way into journalism.

Jiři thought about the story he was working on right now. He felt a thrill race through his body. This was going to be huge. It would be his big break. Once he broke this story, everyone would know his name and recognise his face.

It was completely different from the bland stories he normally had to work on. Protests against the government. The effect of the euro crisis on the common man. The rise in food prices from the perspective of shop owners. Mistakes in the restoration of historic buildings. Jiři always did the stories his bosses asked him to do. He tried to be accurate and creative, bringing some new perspective that no one else had thought of yet. But he had never been as genuinely excited about a story as he was about this one.

This one was important. It was heartrending. It had a human element. It was shocking and worth exposing.

Jiři didn't play pious. He could admit that his desire to stand above the rest of the world drove him just as much as his thirst for knowledge. Yes, he wanted to be a hero. He wasn't one of those workhorses who stayed in the background, content just so long as the truth was revealed. Jiři wanted to be seen. He wanted glory and he wanted praise. He wanted people to remember his name and face just as much as the story he happened to be telling. But for Jiři, truth and fame were not mutually exclusive. They were two sides of the same coin. Telling the truth brought fame and his yearning for fame increased his motivation to work at unearthing the truth.

For the first time in his life, Jiři was doing a story that would have real significance and attract the attention of a wide audience. He had spent months studying parish records and family histories. He had pored over police reports searching for clues and inconsistencies. He had also interviewed people who were so afraid they wouldn't let him show their faces or use their names. Jiři knew the material he had was dangerous, which was why it was so valuable.

Divine, some would say. Devilish, he would say.

Now, the moment was at hand when Jiři needed to move closer to the heart of darkness, literally. He had to find someone to interview who would be willing to speak on camera, even if only as a blurry, anonymous figure with a digitally disguised voice. And he had to see things with his own eyes.

The heat was oppressive. Something in the air seemed to threaten thunder, maybe even a full-on storm, but there were no signs of anything like that in the sky.

Jiři stretched his arms and put on his suit jacket. Over his shoulder, he slung his new black backpack, which contained the thinnest laptop on the market, along with more traditional note-taking materials. He had learned that, with some interviewees, a small notebook and a pen created just the atmosphere of credibility and trust he needed. Tapping away at a keyboard created too much distance between him and his subjects. You had to know how to appear genuinely present in just the right way. You couldn't push or seem too eager. Knowing how to listen patiently was crucial. You had to ask the right questions and be interested, but not intrusive.

Many of the same rules applied to doing a good interview as to hitting on a woman.

Jiři found himself humming. The tune was from Carly Rae Jepsen's irritatingly catchy new song 'Call Me Maybe'.

Perhaps at the end of the day he'd go and sit at a street café and relax, letting an ice-cold beer spill down his throat while he watched the giggling tourist girls and explored what he could get them to say using different interview techniques. Jiři promised himself he could do that if he made significant progress on his story today.

Rules bring safety. Rules create a home. Rules make a family work. Without rules, we would be adrift, at the mercy of our desires, beings drawn to darkness and chaos.

That is why we need rules. Rules are our guardian angels.

The most important rule is this: the family is sacred. Family business is sacred. Family business belongs to no one outside the family. We do not talk about family business. Silence is our rule. If someone tries to ask about internal family business, we do not answer in any way.

For this we all know: he who breaks this most important rule and sins against the Holy Family shall not go unpunished. We shall silence anyone who talks too much. We shall smother all words that attempt to sully the holy whiteness.

If one speaks, we are all in danger.

The will of the one may never outweigh the will of the family.

6

At first Lumikki kept thinking she would get used to this sight, that it wouldn't take her breath away every time, but she was wrong. Prague always looked enchanting from above. Of course, everything looks more beautiful from a height, when your gaze has room to scan the landscape far off into the horizon. Lumikki dreamed that someday she could live in an apartment with windows overlooking a city. What city, she couldn't yet say. During these days in Prague, she had begun increasingly to feel that the city wouldn't necessarily be in Finland. Central Europe was a much more attractive option. You could smell the history in the streets here in a different way. People's steps had a more relaxed pace, and it was easier to melt into the crowd and hide.

For Lumikki, Vyšehrad Fort was one of Prague's most beautiful places. It didn't bother her at all any more that Lenka had suggested meeting here. The hill didn't draw gaggles of tourists in the same way the centre of the city or Prague Castle did. There was no traffic noise. It was peaceful, relaxed and green.

Lumikki sat down on a wooden bench warmed by the sun and filled her lungs and her senses. She closed her eyes. As far as she was concerned, time could stop right now. She could just be here, in the middle of this summer, not wanting to go anywhere or yearning for anyone, as long as she kept her thoughts in check. The hours could glide past unremarked. The day could turn to afternoon and the afternoon could turn to evening. Lumikki could just drift off to sleep and then reawaken to continue gazing at this scenery, which never grew old and always offered new details to find.

Lumikki sensed Lenka's arrival before the rasping of her feet on the gravel path was even audible. She smelled the same medley of scents as the day before, but now something sharp was mixed in. Sweat? That too, but on days this hot, sweat flowed more readily and was more dilute. It didn't smell this strong. No, this was something else.

Lenka stank of fear.

She sat down next to Lumikki. Lumikki kept her eyes closed, and for a moment Lenka said nothing. Lumikki tried to probe how she felt. Did she feel like she was sitting next to her sister? Was this person familiar to her on some deeper level? Was it easy and natural to sit silently side by side?

No.

Lenka was frightened and tense. Lumikki was nervous. She knew she couldn't conclude anything from that, though. This was only the second time they'd met. And Lumikki didn't actually believe she should be able to feel a genetic link. To all intents and purposes, they were two complete strangers.

In Lumikki's life, there had only ever been one person who felt familiar right away, and she was still amazed that had ever happened.

'I wasn't sure you'd come,' Lenka began.

Lumikki opened her eyes. For a few long seconds, the sunlight felt too bright.

'Of course I came,' she said.

Lumikki usually did her best not to meddle in things that weren't her business. This was, though. As much as anything could be.

'I should probably tell you about my family now,' Lenka said.

She hesitated with every word, as if saying them was unpleasant or caused her pain. Burning coals in her mouth. Her gaze darted around even more than the day before. Lumikki thought of a skittish rabbit expecting a fox or hunter to lunge for it at any moment or scared it would step in a trap. Lumikki imagined a snare biting into the rabbit's foot and blood dripping on the white of its pelt. She remembered her dream and shivered.

'When my mother died, I learned for the first time that I had other relatives in Prague. Mother never talked about them. I don't understand why. They are good people.'

Again those words. 'Good people.' It sounded somehow strange to Lumikki. She just couldn't put her finger on why.

'How did you find them?' Lumikki asked.

Lenka shook her head and smiled slightly.

'I didn't. They found me. They came to me the day after the accident and said they would take care of me. That they would take care of everything. And they did. They handled the arrangements for Mother's funeral and all the paperwork and official things. They contacted our landlord and the tax authorities and all the other places I never would have known to

47

call. I wouldn't have survived without them. They saved my life.'

Lenka's smile turned more ethereal; illuminated from within by a strange light that struck Lumikki as otherworldly. It was clear why Lenka would feel as if she'd been saved after an experience like that. She'd been a couple of years younger than Lumikki was now when her mother died. Lumikki wondered how she would have felt if her own parents had died suddenly when she was fifteen. If someone had come to her and promised to take care of everything. She would probably have ended up worshipping them too. At least for a while.

'Are they a couple or . . .?' Lumikki asked. She wasn't clear how many people Lenka was talking about.

'No, they're . . .'

Lenka's sentence trailed off, and Lumikki watched as her expression changed from that bright smile to one of alarm. Lenka looked over Lumikki's shoulder. Lumikki turned to glance behind her and saw a bearded man with dark glasses and white linen clothing. She didn't have time to get a closer look because suddenly Lenka grabbed her firmly by the shoulder, stood up, and roughly dragged Lumikki away.

'Run!' Lenka hissed in Lumikki's ear and sprinted off.

Lumikki didn't wait around to ask questions. She just ran, following Lenka along the cobblestone street towards the Basilica of St Peter and St Paul at the centre of the fort. The rounded stones were treacherous underfoot. Lumikki nearly stumbled over and over. When she took a quick glance back, no one seemed to be following them. Lenka ran ahead surprisingly fast and Lumikki had to struggle to keep up. Lenka ran as if she were used to escaping.

At the church, Lenka finally stopped. Lenka panted heavily. Her eyes were full of panic.

'It must not have been him,' Lenka said. 'He would have come after us. Maybe it was someone else. The sunglasses and everything made it hard to tell.'

Lumikki was lost.

'Before our next wild sprint, it would be nice to know what's going on,' she said.

Lenka wiped the sweat from her brow.

'We're not in any danger. I just didn't want him to find out this way. It would be hard for him to understand. But it wasn't him, so . . .'

Lenka was talking to herself as if Lumikki wasn't even there. Lumikki was getting frustrated. Lenka swung between moods so rapidly it was hard to keep up.

'What are you talking about?' Lumikki asked abruptly.

It worked. Lenka straightened up and came back to the present moment.

'I should probably just take you to meet the family. Openness is the best solution. They'll know what to do.'

Lumikki wasn't at all sure she liked the sound of Lenka's words.

7

The house rose dark and drowsy even in the brightest sunshine of a summer day. It was an old, three-storey wooden house with a tower. Actually, it looked surprisingly similar to Tuulikki Pietilä's model Moomin house. Not the simple, cone-shaped building from the Japanese cartoon versions of the Moomin stories or from the Moominworld amusement park. This was more like the rambling, angular model, with all its windows and balconies, that Lumikki had loved studying as a child when she went to the Moomin Museum at the Tampere City Library.

But where the mysterious passageways and unexpected nooks in the Moomin house excited the imagination, Lenka's family's house seemed strangely melancholy. That was probably because of what poor condition the house was in: peeling paint, rusted gutters, collapsing balconies and unwashed windows, some of which were cracked. The house was almost so far gone it would have been condemned in Finland. Overgrown ivy crept across the walls, climbing all the way to the roof. The colour of the house was probably ivory once, but now it was more an irregular grey.

The yard didn't seem like anyone paid much attention to it either. The grass was short, but it was yellow and dead in places. The only decorative element was the row of white rose bushes along the front walk. And even some of the rose petals were discoloured, their heads hanging down sadly. At the back of the yard was a small, strange stone building whose purpose Lumikki couldn't imagine. It was too narrow to be a tool shed, but didn't look like an outhouse either.

Nothing about the house or the yard was welcoming. Even less so was the massive, black iron fence that surrounded the property, tall and threatening. The sharp spikes conveyed a clear message: don't even try climbing over. The gate was big and heavy and locked.

The house definitely wasn't in the centre of town. Lenka had led Lumikki first by metro, then by bus, and finally a long way on foot before arriving at the house. They were off the beaten track to say the least. There were no residential buildings on the neighbouring lots.

Lenka looked at Lumikki hesitantly.

'Do you believe you're my sister?' she asked.

Lumikki was uncomfortable.

'I don't know,' she replied honestly. 'Everything you said sounds possible, and it would explain a lot, but –'

'You can't come and meet the family if you don't believe,' Lenka said, interrupting Lumikki brusquely.

What the hell was this? Had she brought Lumikki all this way for nothing?

'We have a rule that only relatives can pass these gates,' Lenka explained. 'And that rule is absolute.'

Lenka's gaze was surprisingly steadfast, as if she had suddenly found the inner certainty she'd been missing. As if the proximity of her home gave her the strength to stand a little straighter, to speak in a firmer tone.

Lumikki weighed her answer. She couldn't say that she completely believed Lenka's story. It was a lot to swallow at once. Lumikki had heard so many lies that sounded true in her life that she had been forced to become wary. She had learned that anyone could smile nicely and swear their friendship one moment and then spit in her face the next.

The bullies at school had told her over and over that if she just did what they wanted, the violence and humiliation would stop. But it never did. And they'd drawn other students into their schemes, bribing them to lie to Lumikki about all manner of things. That PE had been cancelled the next day or that the principal had asked Lumikki to come to her office. The moments of mortification when Lumikki realised she had fallen for another one of their traps were burned into her mind.

Don't believe anything you haven't verified yourself.

The dirty windows of the house stared at Lumikki like bleary eyes. She touched the iron gate, which the sun had heated to an almost uncomfortable temperature. Lumikki felt as if she were closer to discovering her family's secret than ever before. If she said she didn't believe she was Lenka's sister now, would she miss her only chance to uncover the truth?

'I –' Lumikki began, but was pulled up short when she saw that a man had appeared at a second-storey window and was looking down at her and Lenka. The man was in his fifties, small with narrow shoulders. His forehead bore deep wrinkles, and his dark eyes glared at them angrily. Lumikki flinched. Lenka followed her gaze and the man quickly retreated. Lenka pulled the gate key out of her bag. She weighed it in her hand, waiting for Lumikki to answer.

Just then, the door to the house flew open and a woman in her sixties marched out wearing the same kind of light-coloured linen clothing as Lenka. A long, simple skirt and long-sleeved shirt. Her grey hair was wound in a neat bun behind her head. Long before she reached them, she started talking to Lenka in rapid, agitated Czech. Now and then, she looked at Lumikki, in her eyes the same antagonism as the man who had appeared in the window. Lenka tried to answer, and from her tone, Lumikki could tell she was trying to defend herself and explain. Grabbing Lumikki, she raised their linked hands up as if to show the woman that they were the same flesh and blood. Lumikki wanted to jerk her hand away. She hated being a pawn.

The older woman did not relent. Her voice rose. Opening the gate, she seized Lenka so hard by the arm that she cried out in pain and released her grip on Lumikki's hand.

'You can't come today,' Lenka whispered to Lumikki.

Lumikki had understood that much. This reception wasn't cold; it was downright icy.

The woman dragged Lenka through the gate and slammed it in Lumikki's face. Then she even made a shooing gesture and hissed something that sounded entirely made up of consonants. Much less would have sufficed. Lumikki knew she wasn't wanted.

Lenka's head hung down in resignation as the woman led her towards the door, keeping her vice grip on Lenka's arm.

53

Suddenly, Lenka looked like a little girl who had received a scolding and knew she was in for a more severe punishment on top of it. She didn't look back. Lumikki shuddered. The situation was strange. Why would a grown woman let herself be treated like that without a single word of protest? It had already been crystal clear to Lumikki that Lenka wasn't a normal twentysomething, but still, such complete submission suggested the woman had an unreasonable degree of influence over her.

Lumikki couldn't stand seeing people oppressed. Her fight response kicked in instantly.

Hoping the older woman didn't happen to be an expert in Nordic languages, she yelled after Lenka. '*I morgon klockan sjutton i slottets trädgård!*' Tomorrow at five in the castle garden.

Lenka still didn't turn, but Lumikki saw her stand just a hair taller. She had heard. After the door slammed with the woman and Lenka inside, Lumikki stood and looked at the building for another few seconds. It looked just as uninviting as it had at first glance. Lumikki decided that, before her time in Prague ended, she would get through that gate and door, and discover the secrets of this house.

SATURDAY, 18 JUNE,
EARLY MORNING

8

Lumikki felt hands fall on her shoulders from behind. She didn't move; she didn't make a sound. This was their game called Be Like You Aren't. The idea of the game was to try to go as long as possible staying silent and passive, without turning around. You could follow the other's movements as they guided you, but you couldn't make any advances yourself. Until you couldn't take it any more and you lost the game.

Warm hands stroked her shoulders. Slowly, they continued down her arms and then back up. Lumikki felt a warmth following the movement of the hands, which now moved to her neck, lightly caressing it. Ripples of cold and hot ran down Lumikki's spine. She already wanted to turn, but forced herself to stay still. The shivers swelled to a hot, rushing sensation when lips brushed Lumikki's neck. A longing sigh almost escaped her lips, but she clenched her teeth and kept quiet.

The hands continued down Lumikki's sides even as the lips on her neck remained torturously featherlight. Suddenly, the hands dove under the hem of her shirt and stopped for a moment at her belly as if considering which direction to go.

Keep going, Lumikki felt like begging. *Up or down. It's all the same as long as you keep going.*

After a moment's hesitation, the hands continued upward and reached Lumikki's bare breasts. At the same time, the lips on her neck began to nibble gently, then more forcefully. Lumikki had to struggle to keep playing the game. She didn't want to give in yet. She knew the longer she waited, the more arousing it would be.

First, the palms caressed the sides of her breasts and then began massaging vigorously. Fingers found Lumikki's nipples, whose hardness made her feelings clear. Lips moved from the back of her neck to kissing, sucking and nibbling the side, making her body feel like pure liquid: steaming, luminous desire.

When one hand stayed on her breast and the other slid down, across her stomach, under the edge of her panties and between her legs, a moan of pleasure escaped Lumikki's lips and she knew she had lost the game.

And what a blissful defeat it was.

Lumikki woke up covered in sweat. She looked at the clock, which said 3:02 a.m. The sheet on top of her was damp, and Lumikki flung it aside. It didn't help. The heat of the sweltering night and the after-effects of her dream held her tight in their grasp.

Why didn't it end? Why didn't it pass?

Lumikki didn't care about the weather. It was what it was. She couldn't do anything about it. But why wouldn't this heartache go away? Why did these dreams torment her? Why did this longing still have her sighing in her sleep even though longing was pointless? It had been a year since then, and the relationship had only lasted one summer. Shouldn't the memory of a single summer have faded by now? Or at least become less immediate and easier to bear?

As the weather had warmed and summer crept to the door and then burst through, the feeling had only grown worse. The summer heat awoke memories in her limbs and in her skin. A light breeze on her bare arm was like a caress. The sun warmed her like the gaze of her beloved. Woken by the summer, her body longed for the touch she'd felt every day a year ago.

Longing was a feeling that was hard to live with. It didn't ask permission. It didn't pay attention to time or place. It was overwhelming and demanding, grasping and selfish. It clouded thoughts or made them too bright, too sharp. Longing demanded unconditional surrender. Lumikki tried to fight it and failed. She didn't want to long and yet she longed. She didn't want to remember, and yet her dreams and her body remembered, reminding her constantly.

The longing was physical. It was dizziness. It was a seizing in her belly. It was the need to wrap her arms around herself alone in bed when there was no one else to do it for her. She felt the longing in fingertips that yearned to stroke, to touch, to caress. The longing made her fingers restless, fiddling with the zipper of her jacket, the strings of her hoodie, fidgeting with whatever little thing happened into her hand. The longing made her teeth bite into her lower lip, leaving it chapped and almost bleeding. She knew she was being stupid. She knew her longing was pointless.

I long for the land that is not.

59

That's the way it was. Lumikki longed for something that was not and which she could not reach. She longed for a person who did not want to be hers. Who claimed he couldn't be hers. A person who had walked out of her life and not looked back. What sense was there in longing for something that wasn't? Lumikki longed for intimacy and trust and sharing, even though, by now, she should have understood with painful clarity that the person she longed for did not have these things to offer her and maybe never had.

Lumikki had just assumed so. She had imagined so. She had wanted it to be so.

Blaze. That was what he had said when Lumikki asked his name.

'Everyone calls me Blaze.'

'Everyone?'

'Everyone.'

So the name issue had been settled. And Blaze did fit him better than his real name. Whatever "real" meant. That wasn't simple or straightforward either. Blaze was equal to his name. Fiery, burning, always in motion, mercurial, shapeshifting, warming, scorching, beautiful to look at but also exuding a vague sense of danger.

'Now just don't tell me you have a tattoo of a flame somewhere that no one gets to see,' Lumikki teased on their first date.

'Worse.'

'No.'

'Yep. I have a whole bunch of fireballs.'

Blaze stared intently at Lumikki over his coffee cup. The gaze of his ice-blue eyes was so intense that Lumikki found herself blushing even though she had no reason to. At least, no reason other than that she had just started wondering where the fireballs might be tattooed on Blaze's body, since she couldn't see them anywhere. His sleeveless shirt ruled out his arms. Maybe his back or belly . . .

Without a word, Blaze started smiling.

'What now?' Lumikki couldn't help asking.

'Your expression.'

Lumikki felt the blush on her cheeks deepening. She couldn't help it, no matter how much it irritated her.

Blaze leaned over the table and bent his neck for her to see them. Lumikki understood instantly.

'Gemini,' she said.

Blaze leaned back, looking at her in amazement.

'How did you know?'

'It's my favourite constellation,' Lumikki replied.

That silenced both of them. It felt as if some strange premonition had lightly brushed by and said that right now, right here, something special was happening. And it wasn't just that they had both independently taken their large coffees black, that they were both wearing red canvas sneakers, or that they both happened to like the same constellation. In that moment, Lumikki sensed that Blaze might be a person who could understand her from half a word.

The first person like that in her life.

Lumikki had been right.

They had breezed through all the normal levels of getting to know each other to a deep, intense connection that left Lumikki gasping for breath. She probably would have been afraid if there had been time. But there wasn't. Everything happened so fast. Her walls all crumbled in a moment with Blaze, blasted to smithereens. Lumikki was completely naked and vulnerable before him, and everything he said or did rocketed towards Lumikki like a bullet, piercing her instantly and exploding into fireworks of joy, warmth and light. She had never experienced anything like it before. It was confusing, startling and unsettling.

They knew things about each other before they even told them. They knew without knowing. They guessed each other's favourite foods. They could predict each other's favourite books. They knew what would make the other cry for joy and what would make them weep in sorrow. They talked over each other, finishing each other's sentences, thinking the same thoughts at the same time, hearing the same song. They moved so exactly on the same wavelength that Lumikki never would have believed it was possible. It almost felt supernatural. It felt like a miracle.

But Lumikki didn't actually think there was anything supernatural about their connection. It was simply that, when they first met they'd sensed an intense sameness in each other that drew them together. They had been able to read things in each other's expressions, gestures and postures that they couldn't necessarily have put into words, but which burned into their consciousness as part of their deeper knowledge of one another. Everything they had experienced, seen, heard, felt, read, tasted and smelled in their lives had left its mark on them.

Everything they'd experienced had accumulated in layers of deep knowledge, which allowed them to intuit their similarity. That was their connection. And when something like that came along, there was no evading it. You just had to accept it.

That was how Lumikki felt. And she didn't even try to protect herself. She opened herself to Blaze. She let him come to her, to wrap her in his heat. Lumikki sensed that she might get burned, but she had taken that risk. She had taken it without a moment's hesitation.

Before Blaze, Lumikki had thought that physical intimacy would cause her the most problems in dating. Years of bullying had left her fearful of being touched, even repulsed by it. She couldn't stand having strangers violate her personal space. Or even really people she knew. She wanted to be able to choose when people touched her and how. Only very rarely did she feel any desire to touch anyone else. Lumikki had once thought that she might not ever be able to date or love anyone, because the thought of letting someone get close enough even to kiss her was so unpleasant.

But when the emotional distance between her and Blaze disappeared so swiftly, physical distance quickly became unbearable. The urgent need for closeness, to have her skin pressed against his, astonished Lumikki. On their third date, they were at Lumikki's apartment, drinking coffee again, as they would so often during their relationship, sitting at her kitchen table talking and laughing. Their drinks always ended up cold long before either of them managed to empty their mug.

Lumikki squeezed her coffee cup with both hands to keep herself from reaching out and touching Blaze's arm, stroking his cheek, running her fingers through his short blond hair. She pressed her lips hard against the rim of the mug even though what she wanted was to press them against his lips. She had never experienced anything like this before. Her pulse raced like crazy. She trembled inside from her head to her toes, trying not to let the trembling show.

Lumikki tried to continue their banter as if nothing was happening. At some point, she no longer had any clue what Blaze was saying. All she could think about was kissing him. About how she would take his face gently but firmly in her hands, look deep into his glittering, icy eyes, and kiss him. Lumikki had never kissed anyone, but now the desire was so strong that she didn't even consider things like whether she would know how or what technique she should use.

Feelings had nothing to do with technique. This feeling was pure burning and fire.

Suddenly, Blaze blushed. He mussed his hair and smiled in his boyish way. Then Lumikki couldn't stand it any more. She set her mug down so hard that the coffee sloshed onto the table. A second later, they were wrapped in each other's arms, awkwardly perched on his chair, then standing in the kitchen, the chair clattering to the floor. Lumikki pressed herself against Blaze with every part of her body she could. Their mouths were one. They burned with each other's heat. Their hands searched for new places to caress.

Everything just happened. Lumikki was simultaneously inside what was happening and somehow outside too. She had no control over her own actions or desires. She couldn't make herself step back. She couldn't have stopped kissing him even if the world were exploding around her. It didn't explode around her, though. It exploded inside of her.

They were rushed, but they also had all the time in the world.

By unspoken agreement, they knew how far they should go. Even though they were greedy for each other, they also knew how to hold back. They could leave part of the experience for next time. And part for the time after that. They were on an expedition without a map or a compass, and neither wanted the discoveries to end too soon. Everything in time.

When they were lying side by side on Lumikki's mattress, waiting for their breathing to steady, Lumikki thought that the journey was just beginning. And she loved that she didn't know where it would end.

And in retrospect, that felt so unfair to her. That her journey with Blaze had gone unfinished. Lumikki knew that they'd had so much more to show each other, so much more to teach each other, so much to experience together.

9

Of course Lumikki had known. From the beginning. At their first meeting, when her gaze locked on Blaze's light blue eyes for a few seconds too long. Afterwards, she could never name any single detail that had given it away. Was it the arc of his jaw? His shoulders, which weren't terribly broad, despite being so muscular? Was it his voice, which was pleasant and deep and yet not as deep as it might have been? His fingers, which were so slender and beautiful? The way he walked, which might have been just a little too assured, a little too masculine?

It wasn't any single characteristic. Blaze really did look like a boy. He was a boy.

But not completely. Not yet. His physical self was on a journey towards oneness with his inner self. Lumikki had understood immediately. And it didn't matter to her at all. To her, Blaze was Blaze from the first moment she saw him, not a boy or someone on the way to being a boy. Not something transitional. He was whole, a perfect individual.

That's why it felt strange when Blaze explained it so haltingly. When it was so difficult for him. Lumikki just wanted to ask him to be quiet, because there wasn't anything to tell. He didn't have to be brave to reveal his secret. For Lumikki, words like 'transgender' and 'reassignment surgery' felt completely foreign. Not because she was afraid of them. It wasn't that. It was because they came from somewhere outside, from people's desire to define and categorise and diagnose, to set boundaries and compartmentalise other people's lives.

For Lumikki, Blaze was Blaze. And at the same time, he was also Laura, the seven-year-old girl smiling her uninhibited smile in the photographs Lumikki found at his parents' cabin when they spent an entire week there that summer, just the two of them.

Seeing the pictures irritated him.

'Can you put those away? I hated my hair like that. How anyone ever got me to wear pigtails I don't know.'

'But you look adorable.'

'I look about as natural as a pet poodle with a bow on its head. It's humiliating.'

Lumikki put the pictures away. But the images stayed with her, and that was why Blaze was also Laura, with those wide smiles and pigtails.

By the same token, Blaze was also Lauri, the legal name he'd have once the physical transition was complete. For Lumikki, all three could be one and the same person without any contradiction. Laura, Lauri, Blaze. For her, there wasn't anything strange or difficult or problematic about it. For Blaze himself, though, it wasn't so easy.

'Since I was a kid, I always felt like there was something wrong with me. That I had the wrong name and the wrong clothes and that I looked all wrong. That I acted all wrong. Or that people looked at me and assumed something, but then I didn't actually feel like I was what they assumed at all.'

'You don't have to care about what other people think.'

'News flash, Lumikki: this world just happens to be full of other people. And we all have to get along with them somehow. Work. Hobbies. Life. And not everyone is as open-minded as you. I would think you'd know that by now. You of all people.'

Blaze looked past Lumikki. Lumikki saw from the tension in his jaw that he was gritting his teeth. Dragging up the bullying she had experienced at school was a little uncalled-for. And besides, that was never about open-mindedness or tolerance. Nothing Lumikki could have done or said would ever have been right in the minds of her tormentors. Being selected as their victim had been pure, cruel chance. The violence had simply been violence. They had wanted to hurt her and break her spirit, and that was that.

Blaze and Lumikki's conversations grew into arguments, and their arguments grew into fights.

They always fell into the same ruts.

Blaze thought Lumikki didn't understand or was being too cavalier about what he was dealing with. Lumikki promised over and over to support Blaze no matter what happened, but Blaze thought she could never understand the pain and agony and emptiness he felt.

'For you, your body has always just been your own. You haven't ever had to think about it,' Blaze argued.

Lumikki admitted that might be true. But why would that stop her from standing by his side?

'I'm probably going to be pretty pissy company during the next stages of the transition. Honestly, I don't know if I'll even be able to stand myself. What I do know is that I can't be responsible for anyone else's happiness. It's better if I'm alone. Otherwise, I'll just end up hurting you for no reason.'

Lumikki soon realised her objections were futile. Blaze had made his decision. He had made his choice and that choice didn't include Lumikki.

Lumikki rolled over onto her stomach on the hostel bed and punched her pillow, which had long since lost its shape. Dark thoughts were burrowing out of the corners of her mind again where Lumikki thought she had swept them away for good.

Where was Blaze right now? Who was he with? Did he already have a new girlfriend who could lie with him on the dock of their cabin, protected from the eyes of prying neighbours? Was he stealing to her side and placing his soft yet strong hand lightly on her stomach, watching her first smile with her eyes closed and then gradually bite her lower lip as her breath quickened – even though Blaze was still doing nothing more than resting his hand on her smooth skin.

Was someone else making Blaze laugh right now? After sparking that fire in his icy eyes that was like joy condensed into light? That thought was difficult for Lumikki to bear. Impossible. It tore her up inside and left a bad taste in her mouth. She knew how irrational her feelings were, but she couldn't help it.

That was what Lumikki hated the most. That she was possessive of a person who had chosen to exile her from his life. She was blindingly jealous, even though she didn't know if Blaze had someone in his life or not. Maybe the uncertainty was the worst thing. If she'd known, she could have been angry or bitter or even sad, but now all she could do was toss and turn in bed and hit her pillow and wonder if maybe, just maybe . . .

Lumikki could always imagine the worst. She could imagine the most beautiful girl in the world with the best-reasoned opinions and the funniest stories and the most elegant manners. Who could make Blaze so giddy with joy and desire and love that he wouldn't even remember being with Lumikki.

Lumikki knew she was torturing herself for nothing. In the morning, everything black would look grey, colourless, trivial and embarrassing again. She would wonder why she'd spent her time obsessing over something so stupid. She would decide never again to be jealous of someone who had no part in her life any more.

But Lumikki also knew that, sometime soon, the nights would come again when nothing could hold back the dark thoughts, and they would wash over her and drown her.

Their last meeting had been at a city park overlooking the lake. The wind was blowing, foreshadowing the coming autumn as it tugged at the leaves of the trees. Some were already yellow. On the peninsula below, where the amusement park stood, whitecaps slapped the shore.

It's a windy summer we're having.

Birk's words from *Ronia, the Robber's Daughter* sparkled in Lumikki's mind. But it wasn't a windy summer. Summer was nearly past. It was ending. The wind also grabbed Blaze's hair, whipping it around. Lumikki knew with painful clarity that she could no longer extend her hand and smooth that hair. The right to touch was denied her now. A distance had grown between them that was colder than the rock on which they sat and wider than the lake stretching in front of them. Lumikki couldn't do anything about it. She couldn't bridge the distance. She couldn't replace it with the warmth that still burned within her. Blaze had closed that door. He wouldn't even meet Lumikki's gaze any more.

They exchanged a few words that last afternoon, but Lumikki remembered the silence best. It wasn't a good, peaceful silence in which they could both be safe. They used to have that kind of silence. This kind was hollow, chilling, squeezing the air from your lungs. It screamed, demanding words to fill the emptiness, but neither of them had those words.

They had used them up. Eaten them. The promises they had never actually spoken, but which had bound them together, had been broken.

Suddenly, Blaze extended his hand and took Lumikki's. Involuntarily, Lumikki flinched as his touch sent millions of electric impulses running from her hand along her arm to every part of her body. Especially her pelvis. *Damn it*. Why did Blaze have to have such power over her? Lumikki automatically closed her eyes, hoping Blaze would do what he used to. That he would lift her hand and turn her inner wrist towards him, pressing his lips to her skin gently but insistently. Nothing made Lumikki go crazy quite as quickly as that did.

Blaze didn't kiss her, though. Lumikki felt something metallic in her palm. She felt it as Blaze closed her fingers around the

71

object and released his grip. Lumikki opened her eyes, lifting her hand and looking at the object. It was a silver brooch with a perfect dragon coiled on it.

'It's for you. Because everyone should have their own personal dragon,' Blaze said quietly.

Tears welled in Lumikki's eyes. She didn't say anything. She couldn't have said anything, even a word of thanks.

She still had the brooch. She could just never look at it. Even so, she remembered its every detail, how its weight felt in her hand, how the cool metal of the delicate scales warmed against her skin.

Her own personal dragon.

But what was she supposed to do with a dragon if the fire was missing from her life?

SATURDAY, 18 JUNE

10

There is no such thing as a benign cult. That was the conclusion Jiři Hašek had come to after months of research. He'd spent many sleepless nights reading studies, reports, personal accounts, biographies and online message boards. In some way or another, they were all dark and disturbing, every last one of them. Even the ones that advocated nothing but love and flowers and fluffy bunnies and peace on earth. Or pretended to. Somewhere in the background, there was always something strange. Greed, sexual abuse, drugs, dangerous rituals, or at the very least strange dietary practices and bad hygiene.

Jiři had studied the signs of a dangerous sect or cult, which included black-and-white thinking, an authoritarian structure and social isolation. Rare was the sect that held together without a powerful, charismatic leader and rigid views on what was good and what was evil, what was right and what was wrong. It was precisely the assurance that their sect's truth was the only truth that kept people in them and made them believe that a better future was reserved for them and them alone. Sometimes in the afterlife, sometimes on another planet. They were the chosen ones. The elect. The ones who would be saved from perdition.

Heaven's Gate was one of the main groups Jiří had researched for background. Founded in the early 1970s by Marshall Applewhite, this American cult combined Christianity and a belief in UFOs. The cult members called each other 'brother' and 'sister', and lived together in a large mansion they rented in California, which they styled as their 'monastery'. Cult members were permitted virtually no contact to speak of with outsiders. Applewhite had himself castrated, and five other members of the sect followed his example. Members of the group believed that aliens from outer space would bring them peace and offer them a home on another planet.

Not that there was anything wrong with that. People could believe whatever they wanted and do whatever they wanted to their own bodies. The story took a tragic turn, though, when Applewhite convinced the others that a spaceship was hiding in the tail of the Hale-Bopp comet and that the souls of the cult members could catch a ride on it. Over a three day period in March, 1997, and under Applewhite's direction, nearly forty members of Heaven's Gate committed suicide.

Unfortunately, Heaven's Gate was far from unique. Jonestown, the Branch Davidians, the Order of the Solar Temple . . . The names sounded gentle, some even beautiful, but all of their stories ended with tragedy and death. Then there were the cults that weren't satisfied with killing their own members and had to look for victims outside. In 1995, a group called Aum Shinrikyo planned and carried out a gas attack in the Tokyo subway, killing twelve people and injuring thousands.

The more information Jiři gathered about these religious sects, the more they repulsed him. If he could play some small part in thwarting the plans of just one of them, he could feel like his work had meant something.

Jiři looked at the man sitting in front of him and wondered when he had lost his faith and decided to break the code of silence. The man's appearance brought to mind an emaciated dog that had been beaten every day of its life. He was frail, his narrow shoulders looking even narrower due to his slouch. His dark eyes constantly scanned the other tables and customers in the café, and Jiři had a hard time keeping the man's attention for more than a few seconds. He looked like he was about fifty, though he was probably only in his forties. Had there been a time when this man really believed that he was one of God's elect? There had to have been. Otherwise, he wouldn't have stayed in the cult all these years.

The man revealed very little about himself. Not his name, of course, but Jiři hadn't expected that. Jiři had received a tip from his boss that the man might possibly be coaxed into doing an anonymous video interview. His boss hadn't divulged how they had made contact with the man, and Jiři hadn't asked. He'd learned it was better not to ask too many questions. If someone offered you a key informant for your big exposé on a golden platter, you didn't start wondering how you got the interview. Grab whatever opportunities come along. That had been a guiding principle in Jiři's life.

'So no one will be able to recognise me?' the man asked for the umpteenth time.

Jiři held in his exasperated sigh and explained patiently:

'That's the whole idea of an anonymous interview. You'll have your back to the camera, and we can even blur your silhouette or dress you in a large hoodie or something to make identification even more difficult. And your voice will be changed completely.'

At the corner table in the dimly lit café, the man nervously clasped his hands as if in prayer and then pulled them apart again, rubbing the back of one hand with a thumb and then picking at his cuticles. Jiři noticed how dry the man's skin was. The cult might have rules about using cosmetic products like hand cream.

'There are twenty of us in all. We live a little outside the city,' the man said in muted tones.

'Where exactly?' Jiři asked.

The man shook his head violently.

'I can't tell you that.'

Maybe not yet, Jiři thought, but he intended to get this man to trust him so completely that he would voluntarily divulge the exact location of the house. Right now, it was best not to press. Jiři moved on to something else.

'How long have you been involved?'

'From the beginning. About twenty years. At first, there were just a few of us, but over the years, we've found new family members.'

'How do you support yourselves? Do you work?'

'Some of us do. Everything we earn is shared and gets used for the common good of the family. No one gets any more than anyone else. When we join the family, we give everything we own to the family.'

'So it's a little like communism?' Jiři asked, trying to lighten the mood.

The man looked at him long and hard. Any attempt at levity was clearly doomed.

'Our life is very austere. We don't need much. Worldly things are all vanity in the end.'

There was a strange mixture of melancholy and pride in his voice. As if he knew he'd spent his best years living in inhumane conditions, but still felt he had been doing right.

Jiři didn't want to rush the man, but he needed something more concrete. So far, he hadn't heard anything particularly alarming, nothing that would indicate he had the makings of the story of the decade on his hands. People had every right to live in communes and spend all their time praying to God. That wasn't a scoop. 'Hey, everybody, look: we've got a bunch of weirdos living here' wasn't the basis for a real story. Not even if people liked gawking at weirdos. The most you could get out of that was a human-interest piece, not a big exposé.

'Do you have children there too?' Jiři finally asked. 'What kind of punishment is used if members of the religion are disobedient?'

'We don't use the word "religion",' the man replied quickly. 'We're a family.'

'Well, let's say "family" then. What we call it doesn't matter,' Jiři said.

'Yes, it does,' the man argued. 'Because we really are a family. The White Family.'

Jiři wrote the words down in his notebook. The name might have some significance. But what mattered even more right now was that, by writing something down, he was demonstrating that he valued what the man was saying. It was all about trust.

'Does your family have any enemies? And I don't just mean spiritual enemies. I mean physical enemies here on earth,' Jiři tried.

There had to be some reason he had been assigned to investigate this cult. Somewhere, there had to be a dark secret he could uncover.

The man glanced around, then leaned in and lowered his voice.

'Actually, here on earth we . . .' the man began.

Just then, someone walked past their table. The man jumped as if a balloon had just popped next to his ear. Jiři glanced at the passerby. Just a girl on her way to the restroom. Short brown hair and a vest top. Not someone he would glance at twice under normal circumstances. And she looked like a tourist, so she probably wouldn't even have understood a single word of their discussion even if she did overhear something.

Still, the atmosphere of trust had been shattered. The man's eyes were full of a fear that Jiři wasn't going to be able to drive away. He knew the man wasn't going to say anything more today. He recognised the panic that made interviewees retreat into their shells.

'Do we have an agreement now that you'll come for the video interview?' Jiři asked. 'Tomorrow?'

The man didn't reply immediately. He hesitated.

Shit. Jiři tried not to let his impatience show. If he applied too much pressure, he might lose everything. The man would bolt and never come back, leaving Jiři with no story at all.

'Twelve o'clock, same place. From here, we'll move to the studio, where no one but me will see the filming.'

Jiři kept his voice matter-of-fact. He tried to sound reassuring. He wasn't asking or suggesting, he was just stating what would happen. He saw how his words and voice calmed the man. The man nodded. Slowly, but still, he nodded. Jiři extended his hand. The man looked at it for a long time, but then he took it. Jiři had to suppress his impulse to flinch at the touch of the man's rough, dry skin. They shook firmly, sealing their agreement.

The man left first, as agreed. Jiři waited five minutes before following. When Jiři stepped out into the hot, bright sunshine, he felt as if he were in another world. He felt like doing a victory dance right there in the street, surrounded by all these cheerful people in their summer clothes. He had his interview. And Jiři was certain that this man had something real to tell.

The woman dabbed the sweat from her brow with a tissue. The oppressive heat had been presaging thunder for days now. The tabloid headlines screamed about a historic heat wave and drought, although in reality, the weather wasn't especially out of the ordinary. Things were just slow on the news front. Usually silence bothered her, but not this time. A long silence would make the scream that broke it that much louder.

The woman looked at the cloudless blue sky. She had just received a phone call asking for confirmation of her instructions. The woman had assured the caller that he had understood correctly. They had plenty of information for now. The source was no longer necessary.

A hero story required danger and death.

The woman looked at the ornate chessboard she kept on her table, despite not actually playing the game. She stroked the head of a pawn with a finger and then knocked it over with a gentle push. Keeping the game moving in the right direction often required sacrificing some pawns.

Sunlight caressed the surface of the Vltava, making the river shimmer and shine. It was a beautiful day to die.

A stooped man walked quickly down the street, glancing around and over his shoulder so methodically it seemed as if no one and nothing could ever sneak up on him. He was crossing a small side street when a grey car sped around the corner as if out of nowhere. He had time to see the car, but not to dodge out of its way.

Many thoughts and feelings raced through his head at once. It felt unfair that this was happening right now, just as he had finally found the courage to speak. He felt sorrow for everyone who would mourn for him.

Afterwards, eyewitnesses gave conflicting accounts. Some of them thought the car braked, some did not. In any case, the nose of the car hit him in the ribs with such force that he arced several yards through the air before slamming down on the cobblestone street. The man's skull hit the pavement and, within moments, a dark red pool of blood began forming under his head. The first Good Samaritan to reach him recognised that the man had died instantly.

The grey car fled the scene and no one got the plate number. One person thought it didn't even have a licence plate. No one had any memory of the driver's appearance or even of whether it was a man or a woman.

11

Lenka walked to the window and looked out on the same landscape she'd known for the past five years. The linden trees, whose leaves changed colour and then fell as the autumn winds came and tugged at them, with bare branches that frosted over in the winter, where buds swelled in the spring, erupting and growing into leaves. Now the trees were thinner than before. Just the day before, Jaro had cut them back with a chainsaw. To Lenka, the pruned lindens looked sadder than usual. The pile of branches beneath them was like a burial mound. Lenka looked at the iron fence that surrounded the yard like a dismal, spiky nightmare. Lost in thought, she stroked the window frame. The white paint was cracked and flaking. The windowpanes needed cleaning. The glowing summer sun revealed the dust and fingerprints. There was no point in cleaning them, though. Not any more.

Suddenly, the room felt too small. The landscape looked confined. Lenka wished she could see further. The familiar musty smell of the house mixed with the sweetness of incense felt suffocating, even though Lenka usually liked it. Usually, it felt safe to her.

Lenka didn't understand what could have happened. For the past five years, she'd been happier than she could have imagined possible. Even though she had mourned her mother and sometimes felt terribly lonely, she'd still been content. Lenka didn't want anything else. She had received so much in her life. She'd received people who cared for her and offered her a home. She'd received a faith that was greater and stronger than she was. Lenka knew what reward awaited her.

Lenka thought of her first fifteen years as a dream she'd woken up from. That awakening had been cruel and harrowing, but it had been all the more necessary for that. Before, Lenka had always imagined that life was only what it looked like. Simple, everyday things like going to school, watching television with her mum at night, daydreaming about friends, falling in love, boys who never gave her a second glance, travelling to New York City, dreams of working as a photographer or a teacher. Life had been shallow and dependent on material and worldly things. Lenka had been excessively concerned about whether she was beautiful. She had stared at her face in the mirror for hours on end, fretting over each and every flaw and using make-up to try to shape herself into something more desirable – even though she was so shy and quiet in social situations that no one would ever have noticed whether she had long, curving eyelashes.

Lenka had been so insecure. She had been a sleepwalker, really. She hadn't been able to see the divine light that shone through the world. Not until the White Family helped her see how small and insignificant all the worldliness surrounding them was compared to the Truth. That she was worthless without holiness and without the one true God. Lenka's life, like the lives of everyone else on earth, was just a climbing of stairs. The true door to their real home would be opened later. So why mourn that the stairs were humble and sometimes hard to ascend when ultimately they didn't mean anything compared to eternity?

Yet now Lenka found herself thinking about everything Lumikki had said about her life in Finland. She thought of the aurora borealis and nights without night. She thought about swimming in a hole chopped in the ice. They sounded like such fascinating, peculiar things. Like something out of a storybook. For five years, Lenka had never dreamed of travelling. Yet now, like a thief in the night, came thoughts of boarding an aeroplane with Lumikki, flying far away to Finland, visiting a sauna, swimming in sparkling lake water and smelling the scent of the birch trees Lumikki described so beautifully. Lumikki had awoken a desire in Lenka to use all of her senses to their fullest at least once in her life.

What pointless, stupid thoughts.

Lenka looked around at the room with its beds lining the walls. Three of them slept here. The wood floor had no rug. The walls had no paintings. No desk, no lamp, no chairs. Nothing superfluous. Nothing that could lead one's thoughts down the wrong path. They didn't need diversions. In the evenings, they could occupy themselves with prayer. If they weren't too connected to the world, they could get closer to God.

Lenka clasped her hands. These thoughts were wrong. She had started wanting something she should not want. She had to ask forgiveness.

She had to pray for strength.

Lenka couldn't help noticing that it was almost half past three. If she wanted to meet Lumikki at five in the garden at the fort, she would have to leave soon. Lenka would do right by not going. Theoretically, she was under house arrest, because she had broken the rules by bringing Lumikki to the family's home without asking permission first. They told Lenka that no one could be allowed to enter so easily. First, the family had to determine whether Lumikki was the kind of person they could trust. Even if she really was Lenka's sister, that was not enough for the family.

Lenka had asked whether the family doubted her story. They said it wasn't about that. It was because members of the family had to protect each other and the holy communion they enjoyed. No one could break that. Lenka's right ring finger gently massaged her left ring finger where for years she'd worn the ring she received from her mother on her fifteenth birthday. Mother had died just a few weeks later. Lenka had always touched the ring when she needed strength or comfort.

But last week, Lenka had removed the ring. Adam had told her more directly than ever before how her mother had lost her faith and abandoned the family, so keeping the ring had felt like an act of treachery. Lenka had thrown the ring in the river. There it could sink just like Mother had sunk.

Now she had to find strength and comfort somewhere else, from her faith and from God.

Lenka's prayer broke off when an anguished, tearful cry came from downstairs.

'Jaro is dead!'

Lenka's clasped hands fell apart. Guilt flooded her as she ran down the stairs. What if God had seen her sinful, worldly dreams and punished her by showing her how easily death could come?

Lumikki sat in the garden of the fort, gazing at the fountain that gushed shining droplets like gems. The drops danced for a moment in the air, but then inexorably fell back to the surface of the water. Lumikki wondered how it would look if the drops suddenly rose towards the sky like tiny, shimmering balloons. And then floated away. She played with the thought of them flying all the way to Finland and raining, warm and gentle, on Blaze's face.

Blaze. Again she found herself thinking about him. Was it the distance? Was it easier to allow herself to long for him when she was in another country? Did that make yearning more permissible?

By all rights, Lumikki's thoughts shouldn't have had room for anything but this strange Lenka girl, her even stranger family and the ultimate question of whether they were actually related. Did Lumikki's father have a secret child in Prague?

Her longing for Blaze didn't comply with traditional logic though. It followed its own paths, and Lumikki couldn't do a thing about it.

Lumikki looked out over the city below her and suddenly felt a powerful sense of unfamiliarity and otherness. She didn't belong here. She was just visiting. She was a tourist who would leave before the city could really start feeling familiar. She was never going to feel at home here.

Where was Lumikki really at home?

Not in Riihimäki with her mum and dad. Not in her apartment in Tampere either, at least not yet. She had nothing that bound her so firmly to any one place that it could actually feel like home.

A hot wind caressed Lumikki's hair, reminding her of how his hand had stroked it and how she'd wanted it never to stop. In Blaze's arms, she had felt at home. In the warmth of his gaze, she had felt safe, alive and whole. She could just be herself. She didn't need to act or hide or edit parts out. She had been happy. She had felt loved.

The wind brought a scent of flowers and trees and summer that was so intoxicating Lumikki had to sit down. The feeling of foreignness and homelessness started to wind its sheer cords around her. It started at her feet, binding them together and then continuing up to her hips, her waist, lashing her arms to her sides, coiling around her neck, smothering her mouth.

What if she never felt at home again without Blaze?

What if she was never able to love anyone again?

What if she had lost the only person she could be truly happy with?

An early morning in July. They had stayed up late talking and neither of them were tired. The sun rose. Its light fell into the bedroom of the cabin, gentle and protective, softened by the branches of the birch tree growing outside the window. They lay on the narrow bed face to face. Blaze looked at Lumikki closely, as was his way. The gaze was not critical. It was warm and full of love.

'Truth or dare, Lumikki,' Blaze said.

'Truth,' Lumikki replied.

'How often do you think about how beautiful you are?'

Lumikki thought this over.

'Honestly? Never.'

And it was true. She'd been told she was ugly so many times that she believed it was true. Back then, she'd thought that might be the reason for what happened. That she was so ugly her tormentors simply had no choice but to spit in her face and hit her all the time. Her appearance was so revolting to them that they couldn't help themselves. Eventually, of course, Lumikki had realised that wasn't true.

Afterwards, she began to think that she wasn't ugly, just nondescript. And it didn't really matter how she looked. She didn't care if anyone thought she was beautiful. Until she met Blaze, that is.

'I was a little afraid of that,' Blaze said. 'So now I'm going to tell you what is beautiful about you.'

He said it so seriously and so formally that Lumikki started laughing.

Blaze looked up and lightly stroked Lumikki's hairline.

'Your forehead. I look at your forehead and I can almost see all the brilliant thoughts running around behind it.'

Blaze's caressing finger continued on to Lumikki's eyebrows.

'Your eyebrows and eyes, together. You have perfectly shaped eyes. And your gaze is so intense that I almost couldn't speak the first time I saw you.'

Lumikki's heart started pounding and her eyes welled up. Blaze's words felt as much like a caress as his hand, finding places inside her to stroke and soothe.

A touch on her cheek. As light as a feather.

'The line of your jaw. Graceful yet strong.'

A finger grazing her lips. Now the touch began radiating more widely, running through her whole body. Deep in her gut. And lower.

'Your lips. You have the most beautiful lips I've ever seen. And softer than any I've ever kissed.'

Lumikki wished that Blaze would kiss her right then, but he continued moving his finger along her neck to her collarbone.

'Your neck is unbelievably graceful. And the way your neck and shoulders meet. Your collarbones are like birds' wings.'

Lumikki's breathing had already sped up. She was astonished by how perfectly the tenderness of his hand and her desire moved in sync. Just as Blaze's words embarrassed her and moved her with wonder and gratitude, his touch filled her with a compulsive, almost animal need. She was beautiful to someone. Someone saw her completely differently than anyone had ever seen her before. It felt so good it hurt.

Blaze's hand continued downward. His breathing wasn't steady any more either as he whispered in Lumikki's ear, 'Your breasts . . .'

After that the words disappeared. Touching continued the tale.

They had another game. It was called Treasure Map. Or actually, there were two versions: Emotional Treasure Map and Physical Treasure Map.

In Emotional Treasure Map, the person in charge of the map wrote words on a piece of paper or drew a picture that had some central significance in their life. From the words and pictures, paths led to other words or pictures. The person following the map got to choose what paths they wanted to follow. The person drawing the map explained how the words or pictures were connected and what story they concealed.

In this way, Lumikki and Blaze were able to reveal their histories to each other piece by piece. Their fears, their hopes, their dreams. The secrets they had never told anyone else. The wishes that were almost too gossamer to put into words.

Emotional Treasure Map opened the strongboxes they'd always kept locked before. They gave each other the keys and said, *Go ahead and open it. I trust you completely.*

Physical Treasure Map also required trust. In this one, the person in charge of the map drew a picture of their body and marked the places they wanted something done to. The map-reader got to choose in what order they moved from place to place and how many times. After the choice of location, the person who drew the map got to say how they wanted that place touched, kissed, bitten or maybe just looked at. The map-reader had to follow the instructions in full.

The treasure maps weren't an end in themselves. They were a gentle game either player could interrupt at any time. They could toss the drawings and letters aside and concentrate on how one situation led to another, naturally and unforced.

There had been a time when everything between Lumikki and Blaze had been right, good and natural. Lumikki often had dreams about that time. Waking up always felt just as violent and wrong.

Why did she have to wake up when the dream was so much better, so much truer?

She had lied. She had told tales that could have been true, but weren't. She had constructed her story carefully and wouldn't get caught.

Was lying so wrong after all? If the lie was more beautiful than the truth? If the lie gave the teller and the hearer more than the truth?

The lie became a story, and the story became true.

She didn't regret doing it.

She wanted to see this story through to the end, to the very last page. She would take the risk that the end might be cruel. Her end.

12

Lumikki looked at the clock on her phone. It was already five and there was no sign of Lenka. She very well might not be coming. The phone felt heavy in Lumikki's hand. As if encouraging her to call her father, to ask him directly. Lumikki was actually considering it. It would have to be a sneak attack. First, she would just chat with him about the weather and whatever else, and then go at him, hit him from behind by asking whether it was true he had a daughter in Prague. She would be able to tell instantly from his voice if he was lying. Or at least Lumikki assumed she would. Maybe her father was a better liar than she thought.

If Lenka was her father's daughter and if everything Lenka said was true, Lumikki knew much less about her father than she had supposed. But did children ever know their parents? Really, deep down inside? Usually, they only saw a piece, just a small fraction. They didn't know what their parents had been like as children or what they dreamed about as teenagers. And even if the parents talked about those things, the stories were always coloured by the simple fact that the parents were telling them to their children.

Besides, Lumikki's family had never talked about things like that. It just wasn't their way. Sometimes, Lumikki felt as if she had spent the first sixteen years of her life living with strangers – acquaintances at best.

It was five past five now. Lumikki stood up from the white wooden bench and stretched her legs a bit. She had walked a lot today. She liked walking, since it allowed her to get a sense of the city better than she could by tram, bus or metro. Lumikki wondered whether she should leave. Her stomach was starting to grumble.

She weighed the phone in her hand. Maybe it was high time to crack their glass wall of silence. Her dad's number was under D for 'Dad'. Lumikki pressed the button before she could take back her decision.

Someone picked up almost immediately. But it wasn't Dad, it was Mum.

'Peter went out for a walk and left his phone,' her mother said. 'Did you have something urgent to talk to him about? I'll tell him to call as soon as he gets home.'

Lumikki felt a headache coming on the instant she heard the concern in her mother's voice.

'No, I . . . I just couldn't remember when it was that Dad was here in Prague,' she said quickly.

The other side of the line went quiet for a few seconds. Now, of course, her mother was going to claim that he'd never been to Prague. That was the only logical answer, because her dad had never breathed a word about visiting the city, not the whole time Lumikki had been planning her trip.

'Have the two of you talked about that? I would have thought

Peter . . . that he wouldn't want to remember that. It's been so many years. Those were . . . bad times.'

Her mother's voice had changed. It was strange. Lumikki had never heard her mother like that. She sounded sad, but also honest and open. As if she'd forgotten for a moment who she was talking to and wanted to say much more. Her mother's defences were much lower than usual. Lumikki had said the right thing.

'Did something happen here?' Lumikki asked, launching another offensive immediately after the first.

There was no turning back now that the door was open a crack.

'No, it wasn't that . . .' her mother said.

Just then, Lumikki heard footsteps on the gravel path. Lenka. Up she ran, out of breath, her eyes red, clearly upset.

'I have to go. Let's talk later,' Lumikki said quickly, hanging up the phone.

The timing wasn't working. There was this secret being uncovered from two directions, but the revelations were colliding and interfering with each other.

'Jaro is dead,' Lenka announced.

'Jaro?'

'One of our family members. A car hit him and he died instantly. He was the one you saw yesterday in the window.'

Tears began trickling from Lenka's eyes. Lumikki handed her a crumpled tissue from her pocket, and Lenka took it with the same submissive yet natural gesture with which a child would take a handkerchief from a parent.

Lumikki remembered the man, his narrow shoulders and the grim, piercing gaze of his dark eyes. And as her memory of his face appeared clearly in her mind, she also recalled where she had seen him today. In a café, talking to a young man writing in a notebook. Lumikki had walked past their table on her way to the restroom. She had observed that someone was doing an interview, but hadn't connected the older man's face with the one she'd seen in the window. Until now.

An interview and a deadly accident on the same day. Lumikki had a feeling it wasn't a coincidence.

13

Height about five feet, ten inches. Hair dark brown, almost black. Eyes brown. Light-coloured, slightly worn jeans that looked like they'd seen just the right amount of wear to signal that they were expensive and had looked that way from the second they passed the cash register. Light-coloured shirt, maybe plaid? Maybe not. Lumikki wasn't sure. Age somewhere between twenty-two and thirty. It was hard to tell with men who had that mix of boyishness and masculinity.

Lumikki gnawed on her cheese baguette as she sat by the river and tried to focus her memory. She knew it wasn't going to be enough. Even if she remembered more, that wouldn't give her any way to find the man who had been interviewing Jaro in such a big city.

And why would she even try? Someone who was a complete stranger to her had been hit by a car. It shouldn't have touched her in any way. But it did. Because if Jaro's death wasn't an accident, then it was possible that Lenka was in danger too somehow. And Lenka might be her sister.

Lumikki hadn't said a word to Lenka about having seen Jaro being interviewed. It was better she not know, at least not yet. There was no point making Lenka any more scared than she already was. And Lumikki could see that she was scared. They'd talked for less than half an hour before Lenka had needed to go back. And most of that time had been taken up by Lumikki doing her best to comfort Lenka, who kept sobbing and repeating illogically that Jaro wasn't supposed to die yet but that it didn't really matter and that everything was still going wrong. Lumikki hadn't managed to get anything more sensible out of her than that.

Lenka had also apologised for not having known what to do to get her family to welcome Lumikki. That would still happen, though. She was sure of it. Lenka had gone too fast, trying to make things happen now, even though she should have learned to be patient. All in good time. The family would welcome Lumikki with open arms. Lumikki didn't tell her how creepy that idea sounded.

Everything got interrupted again, though, when Lenka had to leave. Apparently, she wasn't even supposed to be outside, but seeing Lumikki had felt too important, so she'd had to come.

When Lumikki had asked whether Lenka had a phone, since that would make staying in touch a lot easier, Lenka had said, 'Of course not. That's just vanity.'

They had agreed to meet the next day on Petřín Hill. When Lumikki had asked why they constantly had to keep changing meeting places, Lenka said that it was good not to get too connected to any one place. Lumikki hadn't asked any more. She'd learned by now how strange Lenka's conduct was. She was sure that this odd behaviour had an explanation and that she would be able to find it.

The day began to turn to evening around Lumikki. The temperature was still high, and she could faintly smell her own sweat wafting up from her sleeveless shirt. Tonight, she should at least rinse it in her small bathroom at the hostel and lay it out to dry overnight. She had set off on this trip with as little baggage as possible, and now that was coming back to bite her as her clean clothes ran out. And the thought of shopping with the thousands of other tourists in Prague wasn't terribly inviting. Besides, this trip was turning into something completely different to your normal relaxing holiday.

Lumikki weighed her options. She couldn't go to the Prague police, because what could she say? *Hey, this guy got hit by a car and died, and I saw him earlier that day maybe talking to a reporter. No, I don't know anything about him other than that his name is Jaro and he lives in a big wooden house. The people who live there are kind of strange, but I don't know why they're all living there together. There's a girl who lives with them who might be my sister, or actually my half-sister, but maybe not.* Lumikki would get laughed out the door. Or she'd be thrown in the drunk tank until her hallucinations wore off, or they'd send her out to wander the streets like all the other harmless crazies.

She could have called home and done her best to explain the situation to her father and mother and ask their advice. Any normal person probably would have. Lumikki wasn't normal though, and her family wasn't either. That wasn't how they handled things. And besides, she was pretty sure that her mother would have collected herself after their previous phone conversation and realised she'd said too much. Worst

103

case scenario, they might force Lumikki to come home and she would never get to the bottom of any of this.

So the only option left was to try to figure things out on her own, relying on her own intellect. That's what she'd been doing for most of her life.

Lumikki struggled to remember more. She had to think of some characteristic of the interviewer that would help her find him. Lumikki knew that her brain was constantly recording even the smallest details. She just had to dig them out. No, the interviewer hadn't been wearing a ring. So he wasn't married. That information didn't really do anything for her. His grip on his notebook had been sure and familiar. This hadn't been his first interview. He was probably an experienced journalist.

Lumikki closed her eyes and returned in her mind to the moment when she came out of the restroom. She had passed right by the table. Her gaze had swept along the surface of the notepad. She'd thought how even if she knew Czech, she wouldn't have been able to get anything out of the notes because the man's handwriting was so messy. It had just been a fleeting thought, meaningless in the moment. But as a counterweight to the messy handwriting, there had been something well defined in the notebook. Lumikki had noticed it because of the contrast. What had it been?

Think, think, Lumikki urged herself. A laughing clutch of tourists walked by her. Lumikki kept her eyes shut tight. She couldn't let her mind relax even for a second because she was right on the verge of remembering.

The upper corner of the notebook page. Something tiny. A logo. Of course. It was a company notebook. Lumikki remembered the logo's orange colour and rounded shape. And something else? A symbol? A number. That was it. The number eight. The logo had seemed familiar. She'd seen it somewhere before, but where?

Lumikki opened her eyes.

An orange number eight. Now she saw it clearly in her mind, but she couldn't connect it to anything. She took a long swig from her water bottle and headed off. Maybe she would remember if she walked a bit. Lumikki climbed the stairs from the riverbank to the bridge. At the end of the bridge was a rotating billboard. A smiling woman advertising a new, long-lasting deodorant was just turning away, revealing a poster for yet another cop show. Apparently, people never got tired of watching night after night as someone killed someone else while other people investigated how it had happened.

Lumikki was already continuing on her way when the upper edge of the poster caught her eye. An orange circle with a number eight in the middle.

Of course. Channel eight.

Lumikki knew where the reporter worked.

14

There was so much glass that the building almost looked unreal. The glass reflected the pink, purple and orange of the evening sun, which burned even brighter and more deeply than in the logo. Finding the headquarters of Super8 Media in downtown Prague hadn't been difficult. The rotating logo on the roof of the glass office tower was visible for miles. Lumikki looked through the glass wall into the lobby, where a receptionist was intently focused on painting her nails. Most likely, some of the shifts ran late into the night.

Lumikki had done some quick homework by Googling the company on her phone. She'd found out it was actually a media conglomerate, which not only had a TV station and news production facilities, but also owned a tabloid, several magazines and a raft of websites. Super8 lived up to its name. It had influence.

Lumikki hesitated. She didn't actually have a plan. So she decided to do what she had always found best when she was unsure. Feign complete confidence. It worked in about ninety per cent of cases. Straightening up, she walked through the revolving doors.

The receptionist doing her nails was obviously nonplussed to see a girl standing in front of her with a backpack who had been outside sweating all day. Her expression alone asked Lumikki to leave immediately without the woman actually bothering to open her mouth and say it out loud. Lumikki didn't let the look get to her.

'Excuse me, I'm looking for a man,' Lumikki began in English.

Now the woman's expression changed to one that seemed to say, 'Aren't we all, darling?'

'Unfortunately, I can't remember his name, but I know he works here. We have a meeting scheduled,' Lumikki continued with assurance.

The receptionist looked her up and down, seeming to consider whether to call security. Then she sighed and said, 'You'll have to give me a little more to go on than that. We have quite a few men working here.'

Lumikki described the man with the notepad as precisely as she could. The receptionist's brow wrinkled. Lumikki tried to guess her age, putting it at somewhere between twenty-five and thirty. She looked like a woman who didn't date nearly as much as she wanted, but paid close attention to good-looking men and their marital status.

So Lumikki bit her bottom lip and leaned over the desk, lowering her voice confidentially.

'He was kind of hot. And no wedding ring.'

The receptionist's eyes brightened.

'Then it has to be Jiři! But he's probably already gone for the day. Are you sure that – Oh, wait. Here he comes! Jiři, you have a visitor.'

Lumikki saw the young man stepping out of the lift. Yes, he was the same one Lumikki had seen earlier. He looked at the receptionist and Lumikki in confusion. Then he said something to the receptionist in Czech. The receptionist motioned in Lumikki's direction. The man's brow furrowed. Lumikki knew she had to act fast before they really did call security and have her thrown out.

'I have some news for you about the man you interviewed today. He's dead,' Lumikki said.

That did the trick. Lumikki saw surprise and interest in the eyes of this man called Jiři.

'Let's go somewhere else and have a chat,' he said, taking Lumikki by the arm.

Looking after them wistfully, the receptionist sighed with a shrug and then went back to her nails.

A man put a phone to his ear. He had to call immediately. Those were the instructions. The answer came instantly.

'A young girl just came to get him from the office.'

'A young girl?'

'Yes. She spoke English. Looked like a tourist.'

'Could it be one of his one-night stands?'

'She didn't look like that kind of girl. And besides, she said she knew something about Target One's death.'

The other side of the line was quiet for a few seconds.

'Are you following them?'

'Of course.'

'Good. Let the girl tell him what she knows. That might be just the right move at this stage.'

'And after that?'

'We don't know who this girl is. We can't afford to let anyone foul up the plan now. When they separate, eliminate the girl.'

'Understood.'

The man was about to hang up when the woman gave him one more instruction. 'After you hang up, take a picture of the girl and send it to me and Father. If the girl gets away from you, we'll need to know what she looks like.'

Then the woman hung up before the man could say anything. He stifled the irritated grunt that was already on its way up his throat. 'If the girl gets away from you.' He wasn't in the habit of letting targets get away. His job was to make sure that when a client wanted to stop a target permanently, the target got stopped permanently. He didn't have a reputation as the most reliable contract killer in the city for nothing.

But reliability also meant not getting on edge about how on edge the client was. He always followed instructions precisely, and so, he lifted his phone and pretended to take some pictures of the old buildings and their ornate architecture, although in reality he was photographing the girl with the short hair. He got three good pictures that would make identification easy.

The girl looked young and determined, but not the slightest bit dangerous. Elimination felt excessive. The man's profession did not include questioning orders, though. He felt no pity or compassion for his targets. If he had, he couldn't have done his work any more.

The man sent one of the pictures to his client and the man called the Father. Now if they wished they could see how the girl had looked when she was still alive. She wasn't going to be for long.

Two hours later, when Lumikki sat down on her bed at the hostel, her head was full of thoughts and questions, and her sweaty clothing felt unbearable. She had to get in the shower. Now. Under the cool water it would be easier to think about what Jiři Hašek had told her and consider how it would affect what she did next.

She went into her bathroom and pulled off her shorts, shirt, pants and bra. Pushing the rusty metal plug into the sink, she tossed in her clothes, covered them with water and squirted some hand soap on top. That should deal with the worst of the body odour.

Lumikki already knew the shower was miserly with water, so she didn't let it bother her. The cool, almost cold, water felt good against her skin. It cleared her mind.

Jiři had said that –

Suddenly, Lumikki heard a strange sound. She turned off the water and listened. It was like someone was trying to get into her room using the wrong key. Had some drunk forgotten his room number again? But she didn't hear any grumbling or swearing. Grabbing a towel and wrapping it around herself, Lumikki was just about to march out and deliver a few choice words to whoever was messing with her door when she heard the lock click and the door open quietly. Lumikki froze in place and listened.

Someone was in her room.

The steps were steady and muted. As if someone very purposeful was trying to keep quiet.

A cleaner? Not at this time of night. And besides, cleaners yelled 'Cleaning' or 'Room service' before they came in.

A burglar? That felt more likely. Lumikki hoped he would just take her money and not her passport.

There was no window in the bathroom. No escape. Lumikki focused all her hope on the thief just grabbing whatever he was after and making a run for it. Lumikki knew that hope was in vain when she saw the bathroom door handle start to turn.

A tall, burly man with tanned skin whipped the door open and almost tripped on a towel lying crumpled on the floor. He pulled the shower curtain aside, but there was no one behind it. The man touched the clothing soaking in the sink. He stank of cheap aftershave and man sweat.

Lumikki looked down at the top of his head. He had started balding. He probably didn't even realise it yet himself since the bald spot was still so small in amongst his black hair. Lumikki didn't hold her breath. She knew that, at some point, holding your breath always backfires when you have to exhale uncontrollably, which makes much more noise than steady breathing.

Lumikki held herself perfectly still in the air duct above the bathroom. Fortunately, the one-and-a-half-star hostel had invested just enough in the bathroom ceiling that they'd put up a couple of boards to protect the duct. Lumikki had been able to pull herself up between them.

The man looked around. He even tapped on the walls. He didn't look up. Not yet, at least.

Who the hell was he and what did he want in Lumikki's room?

Lumikki felt a line of water run from her wet hair down her forehead to the tip of her nose. There, the water formed a droplet and dangled precariously. With her hands busy holding herself up, Lumikki couldn't wipe it away. She knew that when the droplet fell, it would hit the man's head, right on his bald spot. Then he would look up.

Lumikki's hands and legs trembled with effort. Staying still was hard. She had to stay still.

Suddenly, that familiar singing started coming down the hall. The partiers from the room next door.

The droplet fell from Lumikki's nose.

The man turned and stepped over to the bathroom door to listen.

The droplet fell without a sound on Lumikki's crumpled towel.

The man waited until the drunken revellers had passed and then slid out.

Lumikki waited as the man's footsteps receded, long enough to be sure he was gone. Then, shaking, she climbed down out of the air vent and collapsed for a few seconds onto her towel on the floor.

The smell of the man still hung in the air, stinging her nostrils.

When Lumikki finally got back on her feet, she went to inspect her belongings. Nothing had been taken. The intruder wasn't a burglar. He had only been looking for one thing, and that one thing had been Lumikki.

Lumikki knew she wasn't safe here any more.

SUNDAY, 19 JUNE,
EARLY MORNING

15

Drip, drip, drip, drip.

Drops of water fell on the pavement. The thin shopping bag must have had a hole or tear in it, which was letting water out. Lumikki had shoved her wet clothes that had been soaking in the sink into this bag and all the rest of her stuff into her backpack as quickly as possible. She had taken only five minutes to pack. Now she stood on the street wondering what to do.

She could try to find another cheap hostel, but would anyone let her in at this time of night? It was already past eleven o'clock. The thought of tramping from hostel to hostel in the hope of finding a free room didn't appeal to her. Neither did spending an hour surfing the internet on her phone or in a café and trying to track down a bed that way.

Suddenly, Lumikki was exhausted. She felt like calling home and asking her parents to buy her a ticket back that same night if there was a flight. She knew she wasn't going to do that, though, because that would rob her of her last shreds of independence. That would just make her a helpless child who couldn't manage on her own.

Right now, part of Lumikki wanted to be a child and have her parents help her run back to Finland. Jump in a taxi, ride to the airport, fly home. Forget Prague. Forget Lenka. Forget that some strange man had invaded her room looking for her. Forget Jiři Hašek and everything he had told her.

Jiři. Crap.

Lumikki pulled her dripping wet shorts out of the shopping bag and shoved her hand in their left pocket. There it was. A business card, badly mangled now. She could still read the phone number, though. Thankfully.

'Call if anything happens. Anything. No matter what time it is.'

That's what Jiři had said. He probably hadn't meant it exactly, but Lumikki knew she didn't have many options now. Returning home wasn't something she was ready to do yet. That would be giving up. Lumikki wasn't a quitter. Besides, that would mean far too many questions from her parents, and she didn't want to be interrogated when she didn't have any answers.

Lumikki keyed in Jiři's number and called. She hoped a sleepy girlfriend wouldn't answer the phone. Based on their previous meeting, she had assumed Jiři was single, but she could be wrong. And who said that single people always spent their nights alone?

He picked up after three rings.

'This is Lumikki Andersson,' Lumikki said.

Then she had to stop and think for a second about how to phrase her question in English, because 'Can I spend the night with you?' might give him the wrong impression.

* * *

As she walked to Jiři's apartment, Lumikki went back over their meeting earlier that evening. Jiři had led her to a popular, bustling café and bought her a Coke. Then he demanded that she tell him everything about herself and how she knew Jaro and especially what she knew about his death. Lumikki told him as vaguely as possible that she was a perfectly normal tourist from Finland and had met this girl named Lenka completely by chance. She didn't mention a word about Lenka believing they were half-sisters. Lumikki didn't think that was any of Jiři's business. Not at this point, at least. Lumikki didn't know anything about Jiři. She didn't know if she could trust him.

Lumikki described catching a glimpse of Jaro and then running into him at the café where Jiři was interviewing him, and how later, when Lenka told her that he'd died, she had started wondering if the accident was really just a coincidence.

'You seem to put very little faith in chance for a girl who got mixed up in all of this by chance,' was Jiři's comment.

Lumikki kept her mouth shut. Jiři emptied his own water glass in a single gulp.

'But you're right. I'm pretty sure Jaro's death wasn't a coincidence.'

Then Jiři really looked at Lumikki, clearly wondering whether he could trust her. Lumikki saw herself through his eyes: a ragged backpacker girl who had appeared at his office out of nowhere with this strange story. Not necessarily the first person you'd choose to confide in. However, the situation was sufficiently strange in every other way, and Jiři was clearly impressed with how few clues Lumikki had needed to find him.

So he decided to trust her.

'How much do you know about the White Family?' Jiři asked.

The White Family. That was the first time Lumikki had heard those words. Lenka had just talked about 'the family'. When Jiři went on to tell her that it was a religious cult he'd been investigating for a while now, Lumikki felt like banging her head on the table. How could she have been so stupid? Why didn't she guess from all the strange things Lenka had said and done? Of course. Now that Jiři said it, it was so obvious.

'Apparently, they believe they're directly related to Jesus. And so everyone in the cult is related to each other. They're not just a spiritual family, they're also a biological family.'

Of course. That fitted perfectly.

'Although,' Jiři continued, 'over the last few months, I've done a lot of genealogical research and it looks like some of the family relationships are pretty tenuous. And I don't mean the blood relationship to Jesus, which is obviously complete bunk – I mean the relationships between the members of the cult in the here and now.'

'Is there a specific reason why you've spent so much time researching them?' Lumikki asked.

Jiři squinted thoughtfully, weighing his words again.

'It's been suggested to me that this cult may have some dangerous plans they intend to implement soon. I still don't know what those plans might be, but I've been trying to find out. And Jaro promised me an anonymous on-camera interview. That's why I have a hard time believing his death was an accident. Especially because there have been unexplained deaths in the cult before. A young person's heart giving out. A perfectly sober person falling into the river at night. A car swerving out of its lane in front of an oncoming truck. A man tripping in front of a train. Police investigations called off for lack of evidence.'

The noise of the café danced around them as they both fell silent for a moment. The surrounding noises came from another, brighter and more carefree world. A bubble full of dark visions surrounded Lumikki and Jiři.

'A lot of them are afraid, Lumikki,' Jiři said, surprising her by correctly pronouncing her name. 'A lot of them are very afraid.'

Lumikki nodded and said that the young woman she knew was afraid too. Lumikki promised to quiz Lenka in more detail. Jiři expressed his hope that they could meet afterwards and trade information. Lumikki agreed.

Now she was standing at the front door of his building, wondering if this was such a good idea after all. Jiři had said on the phone that of course Lumikki could sleep at his place, for the rest of her trip if necessary. Lumikki wasn't in the habit of spending the night in strange men's apartments, though.

Don't trust anyone. That was her motto. Over the past year, she had been forced to bend her principles a lot, and she wasn't sure whether that was a good thing.

Lumikki placed her finger on the buzzer that read 'Hašek' and then pressed long and hard.

Burning wind shakes the trees,
Burning wind along the road.
I heard your voice and I knew
You would burn me,
Would burn my heart.

Lumikki pulled the covers closer and tried to turn off Anna Puu's voice singing in her head. It didn't work. She was lying on a thin guest mattress on Jiři's kitchen floor and knew falling asleep would be hard.

Jiři had tried to insist that Lumikki sleep in the bed and that he could sleep on the floor, but Lumikki wouldn't hear of it.

'Or we could both sleep in the bed,' he'd said, resting his hand on Lumikki's upper back.

Lumikki froze in place, ready to send a quick kick to his groin, grab her things and rush out into the Prague night. Feeling her tension, Jiři quickly removed his hand and started to laugh.

'Hey, it was a joke! We don't even know each other and you're practically still a child. Don't worry. I'm not that kind of guy.'

Lumikki turned and looked Jiři straight in the eyes. He looked sincere. And a little embarrassed. Lumikki understood that Jiři might well be a player, but he wasn't a rapist. And Lumikki was a little girl in his eyes.

They stayed up long into the night talking about the man who had broken into Lumikki's room at the hostel. Jiři was convinced the man was a killer sent by the White Family.

'They want to get rid of you,' he said. 'It's best if we stay together for the rest of your trip. This could get dangerous for you. Although, really, it already is dangerous for you.'

Then they both yawned, looked at each other and burst out laughing. It was so absurd. Talking about mortal danger and then yawning as if it were about as interesting as yesterday morning's leftover oatmeal. It was late, and both of them had had a long day. They decided to continue talking in the morning when their minds were fresh. Lumikki felt like she could have fallen asleep right there in her chair in the middle of a sentence.

Jiři made up Lumikki's bed while she went to wash her face and brush her teeth. Lumikki restrained her desire to peek into Jiři's bathroom cabinets. She'd already imposed upon this man's life quite enough for one day. She shouldn't spy.

When Lumikki finally laid her head on the pillow, she assumed she would fall asleep instantly. She was wrong.

The stars in the sky
Shone down, white
Watching us.

Jiři's joke about sleeping in the same bed had got Lumikki thinking about whether she would ever fall in love again given that she still burned for Blaze the way she did. Because she really did love him. That was why the longing wasn't going away. That was why the yearning wouldn't let her go. Would anyone else flirting ever have the same effect? Would she ever be able to trust anyone enough to let them that close to her, skin to skin? Lumikki didn't know.

One bright, starry August night, they had sat together at one of the wooden stalls on Tammela Square when everything was still good. Lumikki lightly stroked the constellation on Blaze's neck and looked for the same pattern in the sky. When she found it, her mind suddenly filled with peace, certainty and joy.

'I love you,' Lumikki said.

The words came out naturally, so lightly, even though their content was heavier than anything she had ever said before.

123

SUNDAY, 19 JUNE

16

Lumikki had run into plenty of funny words in her life, but 'funicular' was still definitely the funniest. Funicular. Funicular. Funicular. She felt like repeating it over and over to the rhythm of the car. 'Inclined plane railway' didn't sound nearly as fascinating, even though it described the same mode of transport: a rail car pulled by a cable up a steep slope. Lumikki would've flipped a coin to decide whether to walk to the top of Petřín Hill instead of ride, but that morning, when she asked Jiři's opinion, he said that she really should try the funicular at least once while she had the chance. And besides, for some unknown reason, it hadn't started charging tourist prices yet, so you could get up the hill with a normal public transit ticket.

Lumikki and Jiři came up with a plan: Jiři would continue his own research, and even though it wasn't ideal, Lumikki needed to go alone to interview Lenka and try to figure out what the cult was up to. They would meet back at Jiři's place that afternoon to compare notes. Jiři insisted it wasn't safe for Lumikki to stay anywhere but at his apartment. Lumikki had to agree.

Now she gazed at the green slopes of the hillside as the funicular made its slow, steady climb. Her eyes greedily took in the terrain, which was so different to Finland's. Valleys, hills, slopes, stairways and roofs. The variety of the landscape thrilled her. Most of the other passengers were also tourists who kept bouncing up and exclaiming over the beautiful scenery. A few locals sat around looking as morose as Finns on a bus in November. Lumikki had already learned that Praguers weren't the most loquacious or ebullient. Which suited her just fine. When cashiers didn't smile, she didn't have to force one either.

Business was business, smiles were smiles.

It wasn't even ten o'clock yet, but the temperature had already risen uncomfortably. A light breeze blew over the hillside, wafting through the funicular's open windows. For a moment, Lumikki felt as if she were doing what she originally came to Prague to do. She was just another lone tourist no one knew and who knew no one. Free to do and think as she pleased. She wished she could forget she was on her way to meet Lenka.

Opposite her in the car sat a father with two little girls. The girls were about three and five, and clearly sisters. Both wore plaits. The younger had them wrapped in two doughnut shapes around her ears, and the older wore hers in a crown. Just like Lenka. The girls sat side by side with their knees touching. The younger girl had a Hello Kitty plaster on her knee.

Suddenly, Lumikki remembered clumsy but gentle hands pressing a plaster with a picture of Mickey Mouse on her own knee.

A voice that whispered, 'Big sister will blow the owie away.'

And then a strong blowing that left a couple of drops of saliva on her skin. Little Lumikki had laughed.

The memory couldn't be right. Someone might have put a plaster on her knee. Some older friend or cousin. But not a big sister. Lumikki and Lenka had never met before. Seeing the little girls had probably just activated some forgotten childhood memory and Lumikki's mind was mixing in elements from the present. The human brain worked like that. That's how people could be manipulated into creating fake memories, like violence and abuse in their childhoods, even when nothing of the sort had happened.

An even more disturbing image popped into Lumikki's mind. A nightmare she would have preferred not to see. She was trying to put on a plaster, but there was so much blood that it got soaked right through and turned red. There was too much blood. She watched herself start to cry. She didn't understand. Why didn't the plaster make her owie go away?

The funicular jerked to a stop. The jolt was just enough to dislodge the strange images from Lumikki's mind. But at the same time, it brought back a memory too vivid to be an illusion.

Silhouettes of her father and mother hovering somewhere above, presumably above her bed. She was lying down, feeling like an elephant squeezed into a ball. That's what she remembered thinking. Like a heavy ball that couldn't sense its own outlines. Mum and Dad's faces were grey, tired and sad.

'Your big sister . . .' they said.

Each separately and both together. For some reason, they couldn't get any further than that word.

People shoved their way past Lumikki to exit the car. She

got her feet moving too, even though the memory weighed them down. The situation in her memory was real. She was sure of it.

She had a big sister.

The family tree she'd been tracing in her mind had been pruned a little too enthusiastically.

'You really don't know any more than that?' Lumikki asked.

Lenka shook her head.

Her family was made up of Lenka, her mother Hana Havlová, her mother's parents Maria Havlová and Franz Havel, Franz's brother Klaus Havel, and Klaus's son Adam Havel.

'And Adam is the head of your family now?' Lumikki double-checked.

She avoided the word 'cult' for obvious reasons.

'Adam is . . .' Lenka thought for a moment. 'Adam is Father. We all call him Father, even people older than him, because he takes care of us like a father. And for me especially he's like the father I never had.'

'How old is he?'

'I'm not exactly sure. I'd guess about sixty. Why?' Lenka asked.

Without answering, Lumikki shrugged. She felt like quizzing Lenka more about Adam, but she sensed from Lenka's twitching and the tension in her voice that the conversation was already on thin ice and more questions might scare Lenka off.

They were sitting on top of Petřín Hill, watching the hordes of tourists wandering by and marvelling at the iron lookout tower. It looked deceptively similar to its more famous cousin, the Eiffel Tower, but was significantly smaller and somehow more approachable.

Lumikki occasionally glanced at Lenka's thin fingers. Could those fingers have placed a plaster on her knee at some time in the past? What if they had met but Lenka didn't remember it? Or what if Lenka was lying about never having seen Lumikki anywhere but in photographs? But why? That didn't make any sense.

Lumikki thought about how they were here, side by side, so close that their knees could have touched, but at the same time a wall of hidden secrets stood between them. Lumikki hadn't told Lenka anything about Jiři, the man sent to kill her, or any of what Jiři had told her. Likewise, she was sure Lenka was hiding things from her.

Once upon a time, there was a girl with a secret.

Once upon a time, there were two girls with secrets they didn't tell each other.

They were from the same family, a family of secrets.

Lumikki almost snorted out loud.

'And your mother never talked about Adam?' Lumikki asked.

'No. I already said that. I'd never met any of my relatives. My grandparents died before I was born. I didn't even know that my grandfather had a brother, let alone that his brother had a son. I don't understand why Mother never talked about them. She lived with them.'

Lumikki's ears perked up.

'Your mother lived with the family? Before you were born?'

'Yes. But then she left. I can't think of any explanation other than that the darkness went into her. Why else would she have left such good people?'

Lenka looked at Lumikki with wide eyes, as if Lumikki couldn't possibly have an answer. Lumikki shuddered. If Lenka's mother left the cult and cut off all contact with its members, she must have had a good reason. And then, when she died, they came and plucked her daughter like a ripe apple.

'I asked Adam about it once, but he just said that the past is the past and I should forget Mother. He's right. Mother belongs to my old life. The important thing is the future, not the past.'

Lenka turned her face towards the sun, closing her eyes and smiling. She had that illuminated expression that made Lumikki so uneasy. She knew there was no reaching this part of Lenka.

'Is there something special coming in the future?' Lumikki asked cautiously. 'Maybe the near future?'

Lenka opened her eyes and gave Lumikki a sharp look.

'The only people allowed to know the Truth are the family members who believe. You don't believe yet. You don't even believe you're my sister and you don't believe the other things either.'

Lumikki thought for a second. Then another. She began to reconsider her earlier decision. She had thought that she wouldn't tell Lenka what she remembered yet, not so directly, but now it looked like Lenka might stand up and walk out of Lumikki's life without a backwards glance. Lumikki couldn't allow that. It had happened to her too many times before.

Lenka's voice was pure ice in the heat of the sun.

'It might be better if we don't see each other again. You're going home soon to your mother. And your father. Your father. I was stupid to think that he could be my father too. I already have a father: Adam. I already have everything. I don't need anything else.'

No, no, no. Lumikki shouted inside, listening to the two-letter word reverberate in her mind. This wasn't happening. It couldn't. Not again. She couldn't keep letting the most important people in her life slip away.

So Lumikki did something completely out of character. She took Lenka's hands and squeezed them between her own. She looked Lenka straight in the eyes. The distance and chill melted in an instant.

'I do believe you're my sister.'

Lumikki watched as her words sank in. Lenka's hands began to tremble. Tears welled up in her eyes. Lumikki had to swallow a couple of times too. It was as if something black and heavy had been lifted off her chest. Finally. An answer. The truth. It was here.

A group of noisy tourists walked by, but they didn't even notice. The heat and the sweat from the revelation curled the hair on the backs of both their necks, but they didn't feel a thing. They were so alone that it was like being in their own private world.

Lenka hugged Lumikki tightly. Lumikki returned the embrace. She felt Lenka's tears on her shoulder, where they mixed with her equally salty sweat. A startling joy filled Lumikki, the likes of which she hadn't felt since losing Blaze.

Coming to Prague and finding a sister. It was a miracle. It

was a gift. Lumikki had to accept it because there'd never be another chance.

When Lenka pulled back from the hug, Lumikki found herself naturally wiping away Lenka's tears with the back of her hand. Again she had the same strange feeling that she had done the same thing before, even though that didn't seem possible. Maybe sharing the same genes, the same blood flowing in their veins, somehow did bring an innate familiarity. Lumikki had never believed in things like that, but maybe it was time for her to re-examine her assumptions. So much had happened. So many big things.

'I want you to come and meet the family,' Lenka said.

Lumikki wanted that too. Not because of the family, but because of Lenka, so she could make sure she was safe. And if she wasn't safe, if the family was dangerous, she could save her sister.

She had a sister she wanted to save. That thought felt surprisingly good to Lumikki.

'But will they accept me?' she asked.

'We won't give them a choice,' Lenka said and smiled.

Lumikki had never seen her smile so wide before, so happy and free.

Once upon a time, there was a woman with a secret.

Secrets have the important property that they stop being secrets if they are told to outsiders. The Secret is sacred. The Secret must not be defiled by sharing it with anyone who does not understand the Secret.

The woman had told. She thought she wanted to live without the family. She fled. She hid her new name and address from the family. She hid her child. Those were the wrong kind of secrets. Sinful secrets. And sinful secrets are always exposed, sooner or later.

That was why the cold river water embraced the woman. It pulled her to the bottom. The water rocked the woman like a greedy lover. It kissed her lips and forced her mouth open. It filled her mouth and nostrils, entered her lungs and displaced the air. The water wanted her all to itself, as part of its cold kingdom where dark stories are told in quiet, lilting voices.

The woman did not enter the water of her own free will or by accident. She was pushed. Sinners cannot float. They must be made to sink.

And the wrong kinds of secrets must sink with them.

17

On the white plate were two boiled potatoes, two boiled carrots, a slice of meat and a slice of plain bread. Nothing in the meal indicated the use of spices, herbs, or really that anyone had put any effort into making the food taste good or look appetising. Not exactly Lumikki's idea of Sunday lunch.

The food was served in the large dining room next to the kitchen. Lumikki and Lenka had been sent straight to the table, but Lumikki had just enough time to identify three other large rooms on the lower floor. Rickety-looking wooden stairs led up to the second floor. Apparently that was where the bedrooms were. Lumikki hoped she'd get a chance to investigate the house more carefully, but no one was offering a tour quite yet.

'Lunch won't wait,' Lenka had whispered.

Lumikki glanced at the others sitting around the long table. There were about twenty of them. The older ones were probably approaching eighty, the younger ones were just a year or two older than Lenka, who seemed to be the youngest. Everyone's head was bowed for the prayer offered in Czech by Adam Havel, who sat at the head of the table.

The prayer was long and Lumikki didn't understand a word of it. She took advantage of the opportunity to examine the members of the cult, who were all dressed in white, slightly shabby linen garments. They were slender, even thin, which was no wonder if this was their most festive meal of the week. There were no other striking similarities, though – they didn't look obviously related. However, they did all wear the same placid, slightly listless expression. They prayed intently, eyes closed.

Everything in the house was a little tattered and worn. The old wallpaper was peeling and faded in places. The paint on the floorboards was chipped. The windows were cloudy, in serious need of a wash. The few furnishings could have used some fixing up. There were no pictures or paintings on the walls, not a single decoration or anything else unnecessary that might create a feeling of home. Nothing in the house indicated that anyone lived here. It felt as if they were in a deserted, rundown building. Picnicking in an abandoned house.

With his beard and bushy eyebrows, Adam Havel could best be described by the word 'grey'. His hair and beard were grey and even his skin tone was a little greyish. Determining his precise age was difficult, but he might have been in his sixties, as Lenka had guessed. Lumikki couldn't look at him without the strange feeling that his greyness was only a feigned lack of pretension. The purposefulness of his every movement reflected a strong will and a certain menacing quality. He was slim, but the muscles of his arms were well defined. His hands clasped in prayer looked strong enough to strangle the life from a person.

Suddenly, Adam Havel lifted his gaze in the middle of the prayer and his grey eyes locked onto Lumikki. Quickly, Lumikki lowered her own eyes and stared at her lap. There was no reason to make the group's leader any more suspicious of her.

It felt like an absolute miracle that she'd got into the house at all. The same woman who turned Lumikki away last time had stopped them at the gate. Again, Lenka launched into a heated exchange with her in Czech, and again it had looked to Lumikki like she'd made the journey for nothing. Then Adam Havel came out of the house, looked Lumikki over carefully, traded a few words with Lenka and amazingly, they opened the gate.

'What did you say to him?' Lumikki whispered to Lenka.

Lenka shrugged.

'I just said you were my sister and wanted to eat dinner with us. Adam thought that was a good idea.'

Watching the ramrod-straight back of the man walking in front of her from the gate to the house, Lumikki sensed she needed to be very wary of him.

The prayer finally ended and Adam gave the signal to start eating. Around the table, it was perfectly quiet apart from the clink of knives and forks against the plates. All there was to drink was lukewarm water. Lumikki sliced off a piece of potato and a piece of meat and placed them in her mouth. Neither had any salt.

Apparently, Adam noticed Lumikki's expression, because he began explaining in English.

'You may be wondering why our food is so plain. And our lifestyle in general. We believe in all things that are pure and original. Simplicity is our rule. The fewer distractions a person has, the closer he can be to God. That is why we have no televisions, no telephones, no electronic devices and no books. We do not flavour our food. Sometimes we burn incense, but that's only to cleanse our sense of smell. We believe that the human mind is best able to receive the sacred when it is as clean and white as the freshly driven snow.'

Lumikki looked at the members of the family, who nodded solemnly at Adam's words. They didn't look miserable or oppressed. They looked tranquil and close-knit. They clearly believed they had something no one else had. For a fleeting moment, Lumikki envied them.

The group members began speaking to each other in hushed tones.

'What are they talking about?' Lumikki asked Lenka quietly.

'We're reviewing the events of the day. Those who work are talking about that, and the others are describing what they did at home.'

The discussion flowed peacefully. Lumikki studied people's expressions, but concluding anything from them was impossible. No one smiled, no one seemed angry. Did the group's concept of sanctity also include not showing emotions? Or not having emotions?

Once the day's events had apparently been compared, the meal ended in silence. No one asked anything of Lumikki or seemed to comment on her in any way. The mood was dreamlike, simultaneously languid and unnerving. Lumikki tried to make eye contact with Lenka every now and then, but she just stared at her plate.

Once everyone had eaten, Adam said something in Czech and everyone joined hands. An old, slightly shaky man took Lumikki's left hand, and Lenka took her right.

'What is this?' Lumikki whispered.

'The sin circle,' Lenka replied. 'Everyone is going to confess their sins from this week.'

Lumikki didn't have a chance to reply before the confessions began. If the prayer over the food had felt long, the sin circle dragged on for ages. Lumikki couldn't comprehend how such austere, puritanical people had managed to commit enough sins to necessitate these long confessions. At the end of each one, the circle raised their joined hands for a moment and then lowered them again. That must have had something to do with receiving forgiveness for their misdeeds.

Finally, the circle reached Lumikki. She smiled politely, shaking her head and trying to defer to the next person, but that wasn't an option.

'Everyone has to admit their sins,' Adam said gently, training his eyes on Lumikki.

It occurred to Lumikki what surprisingly good English Adam spoke. In fact, she didn't hear any Czech accent at all.

'I don't feel like I've sinned,' Lumikki replied.

'Everyone sins. Every day.' The gentleness had disappeared from Adam's voice.

'If that's true, then it's a personal matter. I don't want to share it with anyone else.'

A young man with a handsome face said something. Adam turned to stare at Lumikki again and translated. 'We don't have personal matters here. We share everything.'

141

The mood around the table had suddenly turned threatening. Everyone's eyes were focused on Lumikki. Lenka looked at her too, but her gaze was pleading and she squeezed Lumikki's hand reassuringly.

Lumikki's neck began to sweat. She didn't like this at all. She wanted to get out of here. Right now.

'Thank you for dinner, but I need to be going now,' she said, and tried to stand up.

However, the grip of the old man sitting next to her was surprisingly strong and he managed to force Lumikki back into her chair. In the meantime, Adam had risen and hurried over to Lumikki in a few long strides. He laid his hand on Lumikki's shoulder, heavy and forceful.

'If you don't want to confess your sins here, you will do it in the sinner's cell,' he said calmly.

'Where?' Lumikki asked, glancing at Lenka, who just shook her head.

'The sinner's cell is for those who need time to contemplate their sins,' Adam said.

Lumikki didn't like the sound of his soft voice. She jerked away and shot up, but several hands seized her as if on command.

'Not the cell!' Lenka screamed.

Lumikki had just enough time to see Lenka's eyes fill with tears before she was carried by her arms and legs out of the dining room, despite fighting back with all her strength. Lenka's eyes seemed to beg for forgiveness.

Adam Havel pulled up the photograph on his smart phone, even though he already knew he was right. It was the same girl. The same short hair and slightly hard, superior expression. What he hadn't guessed was how fiercely she would struggle. It had taken several men to finally subdue her. As soon as Adam saw her at the gate, he'd known she was the one they were supposed to eliminate. Of course he wouldn't do it himself, because that would have startled the others. So he had asked the girl in, and she had walked into the trap like a lamb to the slaughter. Adam had known it would just be a matter of time before she turned difficult and gave him an excuse to put her in the sinner's cell.

Was she really Lenka's sister? Actually, Adam didn't care. He had clear instructions to get rid of her, and that made the issue of lineage moot. Besides, Lenka had always been a bit odd, living more in her imagination than reality. Not that it really bothered Adam. It made Lenka easier to control than her mother, who had fled the family when she got pregnant and tried to live a normal life. That didn't work for the family, though. No one left the family. It was too dangerous for outsiders to know the family's business.

Finding Lenka's mother had turned out to be surprisingly difficult, even though she lived in the same city. It had taken nearly fifteen years, but Adam had finally succeeded in tracking her down, and she'd paid for her sins. Drowning was so appropriate for sinners. Plus, it looked like an accident and was documented as such in the official records.

Adam browsed his phone in the basement, behind a locked door. That was what he always did. Of course, the prohibition on electronic devices didn't apply to him, but the others didn't need to know that. They needed to stay as strong and pure in their faith as possible.

Adam wrote a message saying that the girl could be picked up from the small stone hut in the yard. He would leave the key by the stairs to the back door. The pick-up should be staged to make it look as if the girl had run away, since otherwise the disappearance would cause needless curiosity among the family. He promised to keep the others in the prayer room at the other end of the house for the next hour. Adam sent his message to the woman who would forward it on to the hit man. That was what they had arranged because it was better for the orders to always come from the same source.

For a moment, Adam toyed with the idea of actually confessing all of his evil deeds in the sin circle. Would it make him feel better? Not likely. First, he didn't even believe in the concept of sin. And second, he was pretty sure that he'd only feel better once the job was done and he was far away from here.

The grey rag tied around Lumikki's mouth tasted worse by the minute. Its taste matched its appearance: dusty, nauseating, rancid, filthy. Rough, tightly bound ropes chafed her ankles and wrists.

The sinner's cell lived up to its name. It was a stone hut barely a few feet square that they'd built at the back of the yard. No chair. On the wall, there was only a crucifix and Lumikki's own backpack, which hung on a nail, just high enough that she couldn't reach it with her hands tied. Near the ceiling was a small window through which you could marvel at the blue of the sky. The door was locked from the outside.

Lumikki had already tried for a while to loosen her bonds or find something she could use to rub through them. It was hopeless. Pressing the back of her head against the wall, she rubbed up and down, left and right. The rag bound tightly around her mouth didn't move. It didn't even budge. Lumikki did her best to ignore the taste.

She stood up, even though it was difficult with her ankles bound so tightly. She tried to see how high she could jump. Only a couple of inches. That wouldn't help anything. On her third attempt, she lost her balance and fell, smacking her tail bone against the stone floor. Tears of pain welled up in her eyes.

Lumikki stayed sitting and gathered her strength. She had already wasted too much energy. Controlling her panic was difficult. She had survived all sorts of things, even being trapped in a freezer, but right now she didn't feel like her luck was going to hold. She would never escape.

Lumikki lifted her gaze to the crucifix. Jesus looked back with big, sad eyes. Now, if ever, would probably be a good time to pray. Lumikki didn't pray, though, because she didn't believe anyone would hear.

The sky outside the small window looked achingly beautiful.

Lumikki felt the bland meal she'd just eaten churning in her stomach and trying to come back up. She forced herself to swallow, even though that meant tasting the rag. Worrying about vomiting would only increase the nausea. She had to do something to keep her thoughts and panic in check.

Stand up. Bracing her back against the opposite wall, Lumikki lifted her legs and sent the soles of her feet flying against the door. It didn't budge. Lumikki repeated the attack three times. Nothing. Sitting back down on the floor, she gathered her strength again and thought.

What if she scooted up so her back was against one side wall and her feet were against the other? Would she be able to inch herself up to the backpack, or even the window? Could she break the window or push it open?

Lumikki didn't bother calculating probabilities because she already knew the odds were against her. And probability had never helped her get away from anything before. Lumikki had managed her escapes through persistence, patience and never giving up.

Lumikki didn't want to think about what Adam Havel had in mind for her. And yet she couldn't help herself. She didn't trust him one bit. If Jaro's death hadn't been an accident, as Lumikki firmly believed, then presumably there would be no reason to let her live either. Would he strangle her himself? Or would he send someone else to do it? Would they kill her in the sinner's cell or take her somewhere else for execution?

Death in a sinner's cell. Lumikki had no intention of giving in to that.

She pressed her back hard against the wall, feeling its solid, unrelenting surface. The wall would be her friend now as it supported her. Lumikki focused on getting her bound legs up against the opposite wall. She knew the slow climb up would be difficult and exhausting. She would probably only be able to do it once, so she had to succeed on the first try.

A jump. Lumikki was in the air, her body bridging the two walls. She found her balance and took a deep breath through her nose. She needed as much oxygen as possible in her blood.

Inch by inch. She had to keep the pressure even between her back and the wall, and her feet and the wall. Once her feet were high enough that her centre of gravity threatened to tip too far towards her shoulders and neck, Lumikki started jerking her back upwards. That part was significantly harder than moving her feet. One inch. Two inches.

Lumikki continued the slow, painful movements. The musty taste of the rag only seemed to intensify in her mouth.

A few more inches and her head would be at the level of the backpack. She could knock it off the nail. In the backpack, she had a pocket knife she could use to cut through the ropes.

Just then, she heard steps on the garden path leading to the hut. They stopped at the door. Lumikki inched her feet up too fast, lost her balance and crashed to the floor.

Panic gripped Lumikki as she heard someone turning the key in the lock.

18

The best and most reliable hit man in Prague repeated the instructions he had received.

He would go to the house. Near the back stairs, he would find the key to the hut. He would grab the girl, who would be tied up and helpless, and make it look like she had escaped on her own.

Simple enough. No chance of error or failure.

The target had managed to elude him once already. That wasn't going to happen again.

Lumikki watched as the door opened with painful slowness. She tried to clear her thoughts. Was there some way to trick whoever was coming? What if she pretended to faint? That might give her the element of surprise. It wasn't much, but she had to try something. She had never given up in a fight, and she wasn't about to now.

Lumikki closed her eyes and went limp on the floor.

Someone stepped into the tiny room.

The person placed a hand on Lumikki's head and stroked her hair.

'Lumikki,' a voice whispered.

Lumikki opened her eyes. Lenka.

Quickly, Lenka untied the knots on Lumikki's ropes and pulled the rag from her mouth. Lumikki had to cough quietly for a while before she could draw fresh air into her lungs. It tasted unbelievably good.

'You have to go. Right now. There isn't much time.' Lenka's voice was agitated and full of fear.

Lumikki grabbed her backpack off the nail. 'Not without you,' she said.

Lenka blinked. She seemed to consider her options. Then she glanced over her shoulder towards the house.

'We don't have time to stand here arguing. The others are in the prayer room, but I don't know how long they'll be there. Adam gave me permission to pray in my bedroom, and I knew that he kept the extra key for the sinner's cell in the fireplace. I have to put it back before he notices.'

'But you'll get caught. Adam will punish you.'

'No, I won't. I'll make it look like you escaped. Go already. Run!' Lenka looked hopeless. Her arms and legs trembled.

Lumikki ached to start running. But she was too terrified of the thought of leaving her sister at the mercy of these lunatics. If she left now, would she ever see Lenka again?

'It's dangerous here. Lenka, you don't know . . . I think we don't know the whole truth about Adam,' Lumikki tried.

Lenka took a step back. In an instant, she was so far away.

'Yes I do. He's good to me.'

'Why are you helping me escape then?'

'Because he can be cruel to those who don't see the Truth and I don't want you to suffer.'

Lumikki felt like screaming. Lenka was being so illogical. She felt her slipping further and further away, beyond the reach of Lumikki's words. Between them was a wall.

'But the truth is –' Lumikki tried again.

'Everyone will soon see the Truth and it will burn their eyes. I wish you weren't an outsider, sister, but it looks like your heart isn't open enough after all. Go.'

Lenka's words pierced Lumikki's heart like an ice pick. She could have hugged Lenka and said how truly she feared she was in danger. And how much she already cared about her. She could have done that, but she didn't. Shyness or fear or habit kept her where she was.

Don't ever run after anyone. Don't ever beg for love, friendship or trust.

So Lumikki just quickly touched Lenka's hand in thanks, ran to the back fence and climbed over it, being careful of the spikes. Only once she had run so far that turning back would have been crazy did she curse her stupid principles. Because of them, she might lose her connection to her sister. Because of them, she might lose her sister altogether.

Lumikki stopped to catch her breath and pulled out of her backpack a piece of paper on which Lenka had drawn her stunted family tree.

It was time to go and have a chat with the dead, since she wasn't having much luck with the living.

Lenka shielded her face with one arm and smashed the crucifix against the window with all her might. The glass shattered. The sound would have carried to the house, so she only had a few seconds to act. Fortunately, the prayer room was on the other side of the house, so no one could see into the backyard. The window of the sinner's cell was small and the hole she'd made in it was even smaller, but it was just within the realm of possibility that Lumikki could have fitted through. The ropes were lying on the floor, and Lenka dropped the crucifix next to them. Jesus seemed to look up at her in disappointment.

Forgive me for all my sins, Lenka pleaded silently.

Locking the door from the outside as her heart pounded, Lenka suppressed her constant desire to look behind her. That would have eaten up precious time. Her hands were shaking uncontrollably, but she managed to lock the door. Then she raced around to the other side of the house, hearing as she went how the others were rushing towards the yard.

Lenka prayed no one would think to check her room. She knew that wasn't the sort of thing she was supposed to ask for, but right now she didn't care.

Excited conversation came from the backyard. Lenka begged for strength in her trembling legs and climbed up the fire escape to her room. Carefully, she peeked inside her room. No one. The door was closed. *Good.* And even more importantly, the window she'd left unlatched was still open. Lenka slid inside and only then did she notice that a shard of glass had left a long red scratch along the back of her hand. She pressed her mouth to the scratch and licked away the blood. The taste nauseated her, but now was not a time to be weak. More red droplets erupted from the scratch. Lenka shoved her hand under her blanket and pressed the wound against the bottom sheet. If someone asked about the blood, she could claim her period had started unexpectedly during the night.

The blood flow slowed. Lenka opened the door and ran downstairs.

The fireplace. She had to reach the fireplace. She had to get rid of the extra key as quickly as possible, before Adam or anyone else could suspect her.

Lenka quickly glanced out of the living-room window into the backyard. The others were still there. Adam had opened the sinner's cell door, and Lenka could make out enough of what everyone was saying to tell they were trying to figure out how Lumikki could have escaped. Lenka reached her arm into the fireplace, felt around for the secret nook and replaced the key.

Just then, Adam called for her. Lenka ran to the back door to meet him.

'That so-called sister of yours is missing,' Adam said.

'What?'

Lenka tried to inject her voice with the necessary amount of confusion, indignation and fear. Adam looked her straight in the eyes. Lenka bore his gaze unflinchingly. For the first time in her life. Adam frowned, but Lenka kept her expression sincere and innocent.

'Come and see for yourself if you don't believe me,' Adam suggested.

When he turned his back and started walking ahead of her, Lenka shoved her hand in her pocket. There, both the scratch and her sooty fingertips would be safely hidden.

As she followed, Lenka marvelled at how disconcertingly easy lying really was.

* * *

His phone announced an incoming text. The hit man checked the screen. He was just arriving at the house. The message was from the client: 'Good work.'

He blinked. But he hadn't done the job yet. When he realised what a humiliating phone call he would now have to make, he swore to himself. The thought ate at his insides that this girl had managed to get away from him. Again.

19

The angel rested her head heavily in her hand. A large piece of her left wing had broken off, and her eyes looked as if she she'd been weeping giant black tears for centuries. A guardian angel bitterly reproaching herself for failing at her task. Ivy encircled her feet like chains. The angel would never fly to heaven again with those broken wings. She was eternally condemned to the earth, crying black tears and suffering for the sin of her failure.

Lumikki looked at the angel's sad, discouraged posture. She felt the same way. Just as hopeless. Just as defeated. What had she thought would happen? Vinohrady Cemetery was one of Prague's largest. Finding a needle in a haystack was child's play compared to this.

Lenka had mentioned to Lumikki that her grandparents were buried in this cemetery. She never visited their graves, though. According to Adam, you shouldn't focus on the dead, but on those who were still alive. Lumikki thought it sounded like the leader of their cult just didn't want anyone digging into their ancestries too much. That's why Lumikki had decided to come and see what she could learn from these gravestones.

If she found a hole in Adam's story, she might be able to convince Lenka that she shouldn't stay with the sect. If she could prove that Adam had lied about one thing, Lenka might stop believing his other 'Truths'. Lumikki knew it was a long shot, but right now she couldn't think of anything else to do.

She had to get her sister out from under the influence of the White Family and Adam Havel.

Lumikki had walked all the way to the cemetery from the main metro station downtown, which she now realised had been a mistake. This time, she had taken the precaution of putting on running shoes in the morning, but now it felt like sandals would have been a better choice. Her feet had started sweating through her socks, her heels were chafed and her toes were boiled mush. She had emptied her water bottle half an hour earlier. She was sure she had perspired more liquid than she had taken in during her walk. Her head would start hurting soon.

Her distress wasn't helped by the fact that finding Lenka's grandparents' grave seemed impossible. Besides the cemetery being enormous and Lumikki seeing no order to the arrangement of the graves, even in the middle of a bright, sunshiny afternoon the place was like something out of a grim Gothic fantasy. Old trees reached into the sky, creating strange shadows on the headstones. The greedy teeth of time had gnawed at the stones, crosses, statues and bits of wall: pieces had fallen off them, and some of the statues looked downright grotesque – angels missing a hand, sometimes two, sometimes even their head. The inscriptions on the stones were worn and difficult to read. In many places, ivy covered the ground, the trunks of the trees and the gravestones in a thick, soft mat of dark green.

Lumikki had found any number of Franzes and Marias and even more Havels, and even several Franz Havels and Maria Havlovás. But the dates didn't match. People who lived in the 1700s weren't any help now. She felt the dehydration headache start moving from the back of her head to her temples. Soon it would reach her frontal lobe and run the risk of turning into a full-blown migraine. The Sunday dinner she had eaten with Lenka's 'family' was still churning in her stomach, even though she had managed to get the worst of the dust rag's taste rinsed out of her mouth. Lumikki didn't want to vomit in a cemetery. The dead wouldn't care, but it was disrespectful to the living who came to visit the resting places of their loved ones.

Sitting down on a bench in the shade of the trees, she took some deep, even breaths. Staying here and continuing her search would be a waste of time. She should go to the nearest store, buy herself something cold to drink and ask Jiři later whether he had any information on Lenka's grandparents. Jiři had studied the church records already.

Coming to the cemetery had been a fool's errand. Lumikki decided to take this as a lesson and a reminder. *Don't make hasty plans. Research things in advance.*

Just then, Lumikki's phone rang. Dad. Lumikki would have preferred not to answer right now, but she knew that wouldn't be wise. If she didn't pick up, her mum and dad would just start worrying for no reason.

'You talked to Kaisa earlier today and apparently you got cut off. Were you calling to talk to me?' her father asked.

'Yeah. Um . . . I just wanted to ask what Prague was like for you,' Lumikki replied.

For a moment, she let her gaze rest on the headstone opposite her, which was almost entirely covered in ivy. She couldn't totally regret having taken this fruitless trip to the cemetery. The mood of the place was incredible, like something out of a nightmare or a dream. That by itself made the visit worthwhile.

'How did you know I've been to Prague?' Her father's voice was demanding, almost unfriendly.

Lumikki thought for a moment. She didn't want to reveal everything to her father at once. Not yet.

'A mutual acquaintance. Someone from the past who remembers you.'

'I'm surprised anyone would remember me there after so many years –'

Lumikki didn't let him go any further before getting to the point. 'Why didn't you tell me you'd been here?'

The silence on the other end of the line was so deep and so long that Lumikki started to wonder if the call had dropped.

'To tell you the truth, I was in such a bad place back then that I prefer not to think about it. And I really don't remember much,' her father finally said in a choked voice.

Don't you even remember fathering your eldest daughter? Lumikki felt like screaming into the phone.

'So . . . that's why I didn't tell you. There was nothing to tell.'

Exasperated, Lumikki stared into the middle distance. *Nothing to tell, huh? My only sister, but nothing to tell. No big deal.*

'Well, that's why I called earlier,' Lumikki said. 'That was all.'

'Is everything good there? You have enough money? Is the hostel OK?'

157

Her father had shifted back into his concerned, slightly distant paternal voice.

'Yeah. Everything's fine. I'll be home in a few days.'

Maybe with a sister in tow, Lumikki added silently. Then her dad would get to rethink what fell into the category of 'nothing to tell'.

Lumikki had often thought that her family actually just acted out roles. Mum played the mum, Dad played the dad and Lumikki played the daughter. They all acted as if they were moving around a set, as if they were always on camera. At first, she thought all families were like that, but sometime around her tenth birthday she started watching other families and what they did at the shops or the park or a big family gathering. They acted differently to hers. They fought and they laughed. They were present. They were real. In Lumikki's family, they didn't say what they thought, they said what they assumed they were supposed to say to follow the script.

That made for a strange atmosphere at home and rendered any real conversation almost impossible. In theory, her businessman father and library-information-specialist mother played their roles perfectly. But they still always seemed to be speaking words someone else had written. They weren't whole and living. They were silhouettes. Lumikki didn't know how she could ever reach the real people behind the shadows.

Through the green, tri-lobed leaves, Lumikki noticed that the headstone opposite her bench had a name starting with 'F'. Lumikki decided to check this one last grave. Just this one.

Standing up, Lumikki walked to the headstone and started pulling the tenacious plant away from the letters. 'Franz'. Franz

Havel. And another name. 'Maria Havlová'. Lumikki's heart started pounding. The dates matched.

'Well, call if anything happens,' her father said.

'OK, I will. Bye!'

Lumikki knew she'd ended the call like a petulant teenager, but right now she needed to focus on the stone in front of her. There was a third name. Lumikki's hands trembled as she tore at the ivy.

'Klaus Havel. Born 1940. Died 1952.'

Lumikki stared at the numbers for a few seconds before her aching brain agreed to tell her what was strange about the years.

Klaus Havel had died when he was twelve. It was very, very unlikely that he was Adam Havel's father. Not impossible, but the improbability was so great that Lumikki would have been willing to bet anything that Adam had lied to Lenka. Lumikki pulled out her phone and snapped a picture of the gravestone. She would show it to Lenka. Maybe then she would believe that 'the family' and especially their 'Father' weren't as innocent as she believed.

As Lumikki put her phone back in her pocket, her nostrils picked up a smell that threatened to trigger the migraine she'd been fearing. The acrid stench of sweat and aftershave. The same one she'd smelled the previous night.

Lumikki didn't waste an instant of precious time looking around – she just exploded into a run. And not a split second too soon. Pounding footfalls followed her.

The gravel of the cemetery path crunched under her shoes as Lumikki dashed forward with her pursuer hot on her heels.

At least protect me, she pleaded in her mind to the resigned guardian angel statues that gazed on at her flight with empty eyes. *Spread your wings and raise up a storm to subdue my enemies.*

The hot mass of air didn't budge.

Her pursuer was fast. He was probably much better rested and hydrated than Lumikki, who only had a few hours of sleep behind her, not to mention her gruelling walk to the cemetery. Sweat broke out on her skin, even though she'd have thought she'd already sweated herself dry.

Lumikki rushed past the cemetery gates. Down the street was a metro station. Making a quick decision, she dashed towards it and down the stairs. Going underground with a killer on her heels wasn't the most inviting plan, but she guessed there might be guards there and her pursuer probably wouldn't do anything to her on a crowded metro platform. Heavy footfalls on the stairs told her he wasn't giving up, though.

The train was just pulling up to the platform. Lumikki was one of the first to rush in. Her pursuer had to dodge the people exiting, but that didn't slow him down much. Lumikki continued her flight inside the metro train, moving into the next car. She glanced back as the man shoved people aside and resumed bearing down on her.

Just then, a train arrived at the platform going in the other direction. Its doors slid open and a wave of people changed to the train Lumikki and her pursuer were in. There were dozens of people between them now, and Lumikki watched as the man angrily pushed past them. Apparently, he didn't care that he had an audience. His expression suggested he was ready to kill Lumikki with his bare hands, even with all the other passengers watching.

Lumikki tried to stay as calm as possible. She counted the seconds. She had to make her move at the very last instant.

The man approached. The doors closed. The doors of the train on the opposite tracks were still open. When Lumikki saw them start to close too, she quickly pressed the 'Open' button and rushed out. Sprinting across the platform, she swung her backpack off her back and held it in the air, turning sideways and just squeaking through the crack of the closing train doors.

The first train pulled away. The second train pulled away. Lumikki caught one last glimpse of the man who had been chasing her, red faced and pounding his fists against the window, but in vain. The train accelerated in the opposite direction, as did Lumikki.

Collapsing on a bench, Lumikki wiped the worst of the sweat from her brow with a shaking hand. A boy of about ten sat next to her, staring with undisguised admiration. The boy had a can of Fanta in his hand, which he extended to Lumikki, raising his eyebrows. Lumikki understood it as an offering. She was about to decline, but then changed her mind.

Lukewarm, slightly flat orange soda had never tasted so good.

20

'Did you decide to run a marathon in this heat or something? You look done in.'

Lumikki thought about how in a single day she had discovered a sister, been imprisoned by a cult, left her sister at the mercy of that cult, wandered a cemetery and discovered that Adam was lying, and now escaped a man who had obviously been sent to kill her – again. Banter wasn't on the menu.

When Lumikki's expression didn't crack, Jiři quickly wiped the smile off his own face.

'What happened?' he asked in concern.

'Let's go inside and I'll tell you,' Lumikki replied.

They had arranged to meet at Jiři's apartment at five o'clock. Lumikki had arrived five minutes early, and when no one answered Jiři's door buzzer, she waited outside, looking around constantly.

Before that, Lumikki had ridden around the city on various modes of transit until she was completely sure she had shaken her pursuer. Then she went to a store, bought a litre and a half of water, and drank practically the whole bottle. Her dehydration headache eased and the taste of the rag finally disappeared.

Now Lumikki wanted a shower and a change of clothes. She wanted to rinse her skin clean of everything that had happened during the day, even if she couldn't get any of it out of her mind.

Jiři quickly opened the door and they climbed the stairs in silence. Lumikki didn't want to announce what she had been through to the echoing stairwell, and Jiři didn't push. He knew this was serious. When they arrived at Jiři's floor, Lumikki noticed it first. 'Did you accidentally leave the door open when you left this morning?' she asked.

Jiři strode over to the open door.

'Absolutely not.'

The apartment was complete chaos. Furniture was upended, the contents of all of the cupboards were spread around the floor, all of the drawers were open, the books had been pulled off the shelves, and binders and papers littered the top of the piles. However, the thin HDTV was still in its place, as were Jiři's desktop computer and SLR camera. In other words, this wasn't the work of burglars, because those were the first things they'd take.

Jiři let out a string of curses in Czech.

'Is anything missing?' Lumikki asked as she started collecting her own things.

All she had left in the apartment were clothes and her toiletry bag. The whole day, she had carried around her battered Jo Nesbø novel and her wallet, which had her passport in it. Carrying the paperback had been pointless, since quiet moments to sit down and read seemed to be few and far between on this trip. Lumikki's clothes were all there. The only strange thing was that her bras had been cut open. Did the intruder think she was hiding state secrets in the thin padding?

'There's no way to tell what could be missing in all this mess,' Jiři grunted in reply. 'They were probably looking for something specific. What, I don't know.'

He tossed a duffel bag on the floor, into which he haphazardly shoved clothes, binders and papers.

'It isn't safe for us to stay here,' Jiři explained when he saw Lumikki's inquisitive expression. 'Whoever was here could break in again at any time.'

'Where should we go?' Lumikki asked. She had already packed up her few belongings.

'A place where they have guards at night.'

Lumikki stood concealed behind a tree and waited. She had already been waiting for two hours, but she could wait longer if she had to. She took a drink from her water bottle. Fortunately, it was shady under the trees. When Lumikki had run away from this house earlier in the day, she hadn't dreamed she would be back.

The black iron fence looked like prison bars. A prison. Was that what this cult was for Lenka? Lumikki couldn't be sure, but it seemed that way. Lenka wasn't free to go where she pleased when she pleased, she wasn't free to study or work or associate with other people. She couldn't do what she wanted. And if she had been lured into the White Family through a bogus genealogy, the prison seemed that much more sinister to Lumikki.

She had told Jiři about her find in the cemetery as they had walked towards the Super8 building, where Jiři thought they should spend the next couple of nights.

'According to my information, Adam Havel was born in 1950. There is no way Klaus Havel could be his father if he was only ten years old,' Jiři had said. 'This is exactly the kind of inconsistency their family tree is full of. But the more important piece of information is that Adam is their leader. I've tried to get information about who's in charge from everyone I've interviewed, but so far, no one has dared to reveal his name. I knew Adam Havel was a member, but I didn't know his position. I'll have to take a closer look at his background.'

'And I need to get a message to Lenka.'

'You seem to care a lot about her.'

Lumikki had contented herself with a nod. Yes, she cared about Lenka. She had a sister now, and she had no intention of giving her up.

That's why she had left Jiři digging into Adam Havel's past at Super8 and travelled back to this awful house, deciding to wait until Lenka showed up in the yard.

So far, only the middle-aged woman had been outside. She had watered the white roses with a large, badly rusted watering can. Lumikki had retreated further into the shadows. The woman had raised her head and seemed to be listening, but then she went back to the task at hand.

Lumikki's feet started to go numb from standing in place so long. She shifted her weight from one leg to the other and stretched them carefully. Lenka would have to come out at some point. Lumikki fervently hoped so, at least.

Finally, the back door opened and Lumikki saw that familiar crown of braids. Lenka. She looked sad, somehow even more beaten down. Lumikki let out a low whistle. Lenka looked in her direction and made eye contact. Lumikki quickly lifted a finger to her lips. They couldn't take the risk of the other residents of the house seeing her. Lenka looked around hesitantly and then walked closer to the iron fence. She made a slight motion with her head towards the house and then shook her head almost imperceptibly. Lumikki understood from the sign that Lenka couldn't go beyond the yard.

Fortunately, Lumikki was prepared. She flashed a piece of paper at Lenka, which she had written a message on, then she crumpled it up and tossed it over the fence. It landed just a few feet from Lenka.

Just then, the back door opened and a young man came out. Lenka swiftly sidestepped and scooted one foot on the paper ball without looking down. The man yelled something at Lenka. Lenka answered. The man's tone turned impatient, but Lenka just shrugged. The man sighed, made one more sharp comment and then went back inside. Quickly crouching, Lenka picked up the paper and hid it in her pocket. Then she cast a last glance at Lumikki and went inside.

Lumikki released the air from her lungs. She had been holding her breath without realising it.

The message she had written said that she wanted to meet Lenka the next day at twelve o'clock at the same place they first talked. Lumikki trusted that Lenka could come up with some way to slip out by then.

Lumikki's feet felt strangely heavy as she set off back to the city centre. Sweat ran down her back in rivulets. When she licked her lips, the taste of salt was strong and biting.

* * *

The long summer day was finally winding down and the sky had turned blue-black. The lights of the city reflected off the large glass windows of the Super8 building. From the ninth floor, Lumikki could see the whole city, all the way to the castle, lit up beautifully like it was every night. Lumikki fought to keep her eyes open. She was so tired she was afraid she might fall asleep sitting up.

Jiři had spread out two camping mats in one corner of the office and even found them sleeping bags.

'Good thing the company has a mountaineering division,' he said with a grin.

Apparently, that wasn't a joke.

Jiři's computer glowed with a blue light. He had been sitting at it without moving for the past three hours. Before that, he had only moved once to accept the cardboard takeaway boxes the delivery boy from the Chinese restaurant had brought. He'd assigned Lumikki to go over the family records, which were full of Jiři's annotations, question marks and arrows. Lumikki hadn't found any new earth-shattering secrets.

She decided to close her eyes just for a second. Just to rest them. The day had been so long. If she just closed her eyes for a second or two . . .

Lumikki woke up when her forehead hit the stack of paper. Jiři looked up.

'You should go to sleep. You've had a rough day.'

'I'm fine,' Lumikki said, just as her mouth stretched wide in a yawn.

'Or eat some chilli tofu. That'll wake you up.'

Jiři pushed a takeaway box across the desk.

'Cold tofu? Thanks for the offer, but I think I'll hold off on that gourmet experience,' Lumikki replied. 'Besides, I'm still stuffed. You ordered enough food for three people.'

'Your choice. But then don't – bingo!'

Jiři yelled the last word so loudly that Lumikki jumped in her seat.

'Come and look!'

Lumikki came around the desk to see. On the computer screen was a picture of a man of about thirty dressed in a well-cut white linen outfit. His long hair was pulled back in a tight ponytail. Lumikki recognised the piercing grey eyes and bushy, almost owlish eyebrows even though he was much younger in the picture.

'Adam Havel,' Lumikki said.

'Actually, Adam Smith. Alias Adam Havel. This picture is from 1980, but even I recognise him, and I've only ever heard descriptions of what he looks like,' Jiři explained excitedly.

'Nebraska,' Lumikki read from the caption.

'Exactly. There was a cult there called the White Brothers. They only admitted young men as members and claimed they were all related to Jesus. The group's leader was Adam Smith, but he disappeared – as it turns out, only to appear later in Prague using basically the same concept. This time he just decided to include women too.'

'Why did he disappear?' Lumikki asked.

'He convinced the other members of the cult to turn over all their property to him, which he was supposedly going to donate to charity. So they would be as pure as possible when they met their death.'

Jiři looked at Lumikki, his face darkening.

'They were going to commit mass suicide. Adam Smith along with the rest of them. But then someone tipped off the police, who managed to save most of them. They found them lying in a cabin, unconscious from carbon monoxide poisoning. Adam Smith was gone. With the money, of course.'

Suddenly, Lumikki's drowsiness had vanished.

'The White Family isn't planning an attack on anyone,' she said slowly.

Jiři shook his head.

Neither of them had to say it out loud. Still, the words surrounded them, cold as ice. Mass suicide.

MONDAY, 20 JUNE

21

Lumikki checked her phone: 11:45 a.m. She could still make it to their meeting place on time if she hurried.

She and Jiři had agreed that Lumikki would go and meet Lenka and try to get her to leave the cult immediately. It was also important to find out if the date for the suicide was already set. Jiři had a meeting at the same time with the boss at Super8 who had assigned him the story about the cult in the first place.

Lumikki understood too late what was happening when strong hands pulled her off the street and into a car, and shoved her against the back seat. The cold muzzle of a gun kissed her neck.

'If you try anything or make one single sound, you're dead,' the man hissed in her ear.

Lumikki hadn't been this close to her pursuer, and she would have preferred to keep it that way. She saw his other hand fumbling with a roll of duct tape. Lumikki guessed he was going to put tape over her mouth, tape her wrists and ankles together, and then drive somewhere far away from anyone to do whatever he intended.

Lumikki didn't want to find out what that was. Burning rage flared inside of her. Once again, she had been dragged into the middle of something she didn't want anything to do with. Entirely without her consent.

There was no time to waste. She had to act. Taking advantage of the element of surprise was only possible for a brief moment.

Lumikki pretended to nod that she understood. But instead, quick as a flash, she continued the motion and struck the man in the nose with her forehead. The man's grip loosened, more from surprise than pain, as his nose spurted blood onto Lumikki's white cotton shirt.

Lumikki tore herself away, got the vehicle door open and tumbled out into the street. As she darted forward, it wasn't until the crowds grew thicker that she realised she must be near the Charles Bridge, which drew Prague tourists like a giant magnet. Near the bridge, the throng became even thicker. People stood on the spot, staring up, as Lumikki tried desperately to get past them. What on earth were they waiting for?

Lumikki glanced up, and then she understood. A bugle player had appeared on a balcony of a nearby building, just beginning to announce the twelve o'clock hour. The mouth of the bridge was distressingly packed with people. Lumikki looked back. Had she managed to lose her pursuer? She couldn't see him. Lumikki moved further into the crowd to hide. Her heart pounded alarmingly.

Suddenly, Lumikki heard a sound behind her. Looking over her shoulder, she caught a glimpse of the man some distance away, but not far enough. He spotted her too and shoved a few old ladies out of the way, who began screaming curses at him in French.

174

Lumikki's mind raced. Should she try to get away across the crowded bridge or continue along the same side of the riverbank? Making any headway on the bridge might be impossible. On the other hand, her pursuer would have the same problem. And maybe he wouldn't dare attack her or shoot at her on the bridge. There would be too many witnesses.

She had made her decision. Lumikki crouched to slip under the arm of a Japanese tourist just as he raised it to get a mobile phone picture of the bugler. She heard but didn't see as, a few seconds later, the hit man collided with the tourist and the phone went flying through the air onto the cobblestones. Based on the Japanese man's agitated protestations, the phone didn't survive.

The statues of thirty saints stood guard on the sides of the bridge. Saint John of Nepomuk, Saint Vitus, Saint Luthgard, John the Baptist, Saint Wenceslas, Saint Sigismund, Saint Jude Thaddeus, Francis of Assisi. The names listed in the travel guide ran through Lumikki's mind in time with the thudding of her feet on the stone pavement of the bridge. The Stone Bridge. That was its original name. The imagination of whoever had named it had run absolutely wild.

Salty, stinging sweat ran into Lumikki's eyes and she swiped at them with the back of her hand. She wouldn't be able to run on the bridge blind. Dodging the tourists, kitsch vendors and street musicians was hard enough as it was. Her sandals rubbed her feet raw. They weren't running shoes, and her soaking wet cotton shirt wasn't a running shirt. Eighty-five degrees also wasn't the best possible running weather, but Lumikki couldn't change the conditions now. She just had to keep moving and try to get away.

The man was keeping up with her, only a few yards behind now.

And their chase was attracting attention. The tourists thought it was some kind of performance. Some shouted words of encouragement to Lumikki, and others cheered for her pursuer.

A quintet playing a dramatic opera score faltered as Lumikki dashed past them. She heard them switch on the fly to a lighter piece. The Beatles' 'Run for Your Life'.

Thanks. I actually am running for my life here, Lumikki managed to think just before she collided with a plump German woman who'd stepped to the side at just the wrong moment.

'*Mein Gott!*' the woman exclaimed.

'*Entschuldigung!*' Lumikki dug out from somewhere in her vocabulary and continued running.

Luckily, the German woman also slowed her pursuer, who shoved her roughly aside without an apology in any language.

As she struggled to speed up and felt the sweat streaming down her calves, Lumikki found she could no longer weave through the crowds of people as well as she had at first.

A Japanese bride was being photographed in the middle of the bridge. Lumikki wasn't sure whether the photoshoot was genuine or staged. The bride's gown had an insanely impractical long train, which Lumikki had to vault over at the last moment. A couple of seconds later, the sound of ripping satin revealed that her pursuer hadn't been so nimble.

Lumikki gained a small lead.

Next to block her way was a group of Americans with a tour guide. Lumikki looked at the wall of people in horror, but then saw one narrow break she just managed to slip through sideways.

'And as you can see, here we have a statue of a – running girl – I mean –'

Lumikki didn't hang around to hear how the guide got his commentary back on track. The hit man had charged through the wall of Americans like an ice-breaker and shrunk her lead to almost nothing. Lumikki felt the heat threatening to cloud her mind. Her mouth was bone-dry. She felt as if she'd never drunk a drop of water in her life.

Lumikki felt a tremor in her legs. Her elbow bumped a caricature artist's hand just as he was sketching the nose of a man with a dark beard. Well, a bolder nose would probably improve the picture. The crush of people forced Lumikki to the side of the bridge. She had to reach out and push off a statue's plaque to avoid ramming her side painfully into the railing. The metal plate was shiny from thousands of people touching it. Saint John of Nepomuk. A sainted Czech martyr who was executed by being thrown off a bridge. You never knew what little things would stick in your head from reading a travel guide. Lumikki also remembered that touching the statue was said to bring good luck and ensure that the person would return to Prague again one day.

Good luck was just what she needed now. She heard her pursuer's heavy breathing, and it was far too close. On the other hand, she wasn't at all sure she'd ever want to come back to Prague if she made it out alive.

Lumikki was almost at the other end of the bridge already. Her heart was banging against her ribs, trying desperately to pump oxygen to her muscles, which were on the verge of complete collapse. Lumikki felt so hot it was like her whole body was boiling.

A glass player. It couldn't be true. Ahead of her, Lumikki saw an old, frail man intently playing dozens of equally fragile-looking wine glasses arranged in three levels in front of him. Lumikki strained with all her might, concentrating her balance to dodge to the left around the man and pass him safely without breaking a single glass.

The old man, as if made from frosted glass himself, raised his hand in thanks.

A moment too soon.

Behind her Lumikki heard her pursuer's heavy steps approach and the old man cry out as first one glass and then a second, a third and a forth shattered. The domino effect sent each breaking glass tumbling into the next, causing a new explosion of shards. Lumikki's pursuer screamed and cursed. It was clear he'd injured himself and lost significant ground.

Lumikki rushed off the bridge, vowing never to cross it again by choice.

The knowledge that her pursuer probably wouldn't be able to catch up with her now instantly made Lumikki feel better. Her legs found new strength, and the hot air didn't parch her lungs. She couldn't feel the blisters caused by her sandals, and the flow of sweat was pleasantly cooling.

She ran to the stairs leading to Saint Vitus Cathedral and started loping up them two at a time. The joy of escape gave her heels wings. She would be late for her rendezvous by a few minutes, but she would make it there alive. That hadn't been a given.

'Go, go, go!' some young boys sitting on the stairs yelled in encouragement.

She glanced back, even though she was already sure. No one was following.

Now she just hoped Lenka would be waiting for her.

22

Two little girls looked back from the mirror. One larger, one smaller. Sisters. They held each other by the hand.

The vision faded before Lumikki's eyes. Now, in the mirror, she saw herself and Lenka. They had come to the women's restroom at the same café from their first meeting. Lumikki figured this wouldn't be the first place her pursuer would think to look for them, even if he somehow managed to track her here. And he probably wouldn't take the risk of attracting attention by marching into the ladies' room.

Lumikki's shirt looked grotesque. Red on white. She could have come straight from a slaughterhouse. The barista at the café had looked at her with raised eyebrows, but apparently Lumikki's expression had been sufficiently grim that the woman had decided not to say anything.

Lenka shook her head and tears ran down her cheeks.

'I can't leave,' she said.

She had been repeating this refrain the whole time, even though Lumikki had tried to convince her that if Lenka didn't go with her now, she might die.

'Your life will be in danger if you go back there. Adam is

insane and he's going to kill all of you.'

Lumikki tried to keep her voice steady, even though she wanted to scream the words.

'We shall receive eternal life,' Lenka argued.

In frustration, Lumikki slammed her palms on the sink counter.

How were you supposed to talk to these brainwashed lunatics so they would understand?

'You probably will receive eternal life if that's what you believe,' Lumikki sighed. 'But what's the rush? You'll still get it in sixty years when you've lived a long, full life and then die happily of old age.'

'I can't decide the time of my death. I have to accept whatever comes from above,' Lenka said. The words came mechanically, like a recording that had been played many times.

'You don't have to. You can make your own decisions.'

'If I leave, I won't have anything. I don't have anything. I don't have anyone.'

Lumikki took Lenka's hand. In the mirror, she looked her straight in the eyes.

'You have me. These cult members aren't even related to you. I'm your sister. I'll help you.'

Lenka just shook her head and wept even more uncontrollably.

'No. It's not true,' she said.

'It is. I promise you.'

'No, it isn't. I lied to you. I made up the whole sister story. It's a fairy tale.'

Lumikki let go of Lenka's hand. Suddenly, she felt weak. She hadn't seen this coming. Not that Lenka had lied to her, and especially not how bad it felt. Suddenly, with one sentence,

181

the decisive piece of the puzzle that was her past had been snatched away, and the hole it left behind felt bigger and emptier than ever before. Only now did Lumikki understand how deeply she had hoped Lenka would help her uncover the secret her family was hiding.

Her sister had been taken away.

'I spied on you,' Lenka said.

'Why?' Lumikki asked.

Now she was the one who sounded like a machine. A veil lay over her thoughts, but her mouth apparently still produced intelligible words.

'I knew my father spoke Swedish. Mother told me that. But she wouldn't say anything else about him. Not even his name. And I overheard you speaking Swedish to some tourists.'

Lumikki remembered. A group of Swedish retirees had tried to ask her directions in halting English, so Lumikki took pity on them and replied in Swedish, which made the grannies and grandpas so overjoyed that they wanted to buy her ice cream. Lumikki declined. She didn't want to get roped into acting as their tour guide and map-reader.

'I followed you and got your name from the hostel. I eavesdropped on you when you were talking on the phone to someone you first called "Peter" and then "Dad".'

Lumikki remembered the call too. Her dad had answered the phone so formally – 'Peter Andersson here' – that Lumikki had repeated it teasingly in the same tone of voice. Her dad had explained that he hadn't been able to see the caller's name on his phone in the bright sunlight, and that was why he had answered that way.

'But why?' Lumikki managed to ask. The words nearly stuck in her throat.

She couldn't remember anyone ever having lied to her so successfully. Maybe she had just wanted to find that missing puzzle piece too much.

'Because I don't actually have anyone close to me in the White Family. Everyone else has someone who's more "theirs" than anyone else's. And I've always wanted a sister. I thought that if I had a sister I wouldn't be so alone. Even a made-up sister. I've been building the story of having a sister for years. It felt so true I almost started believing it myself. And when I saw you, I knew instantly. You're my fairy-tale sister.'

Lumikki listened to Lenka's words and understood them, but she felt completely cold. All she could think about was how Lenka had betrayed her.

Lumikki didn't say anything. Lenka was silent. Two young women in the mirror. Complete strangers.

'So you understand now that I really don't have anyone or anything. Nothing but the White Family and my faith.'

Lumikki didn't have the energy to argue any more. She didn't have the energy to try to convince Lenka. Let her do whatever she wanted. It was none of Lumikki's business. It never had been.

Lenka touched Lumikki lightly on the shoulder and walked out. Lumikki didn't even glance after her.

She just stood there staring at herself and her bloodstained shirt. She remembered her dream. The bloody tears. *Du är min syster*. Had that just been a fairy tale too? A nightmare? A lie?

* * *

The woman grabbed the mobile phone. There was no time to waste. When the other side picked up, she got straight to the point.

'The girl is still in the game. And she might ruin everything. We have to move up the schedule. It has to happen today.'

'Today? I'm not sure we can –'

'We can. We have to. The machinery is all in place. I can set it in motion any time. You just have to be able to handle your part. Just say you received a commandment from a higher power. Then you aren't even lying.'

'Lying has never been a problem for me.'

'We're different that way. I don't want to tell lies. I want to tell true stories. They're more interesting.'

'And I lie to give you your true story.'

'That's what you're paid for.'

'Maybe in this life, but what about on the other side?'

'Who wants to think that far ahead?'

'Fine. So, today. Theoretically, everything is ready. All we need is a little spark –'

'– and the bonfire will ignite. Just like it should. Seven o'clock sharp?'

'Sounds good.'

Vera Sováková stroked the surface of her desk. The evening news would be full of this and only this. On her channel first and foremost. With the deepest, most thorough coverage. And the next day in the newspapers – her newspapers. For weeks to come. Big pictures, tears, in-depth interviews, expert analysis. An unimaginable tragedy with only a tiny glimmer of hope. A hero story.

She didn't worry about whether her actions were immoral. Of course they were. But morality didn't sell newspapers, and especially not advertising space. The more readers and viewers, the more advertisements and the more ad money to make even better news. Even bigger and more touching stories for people who hungered for emotion and excitement. Not from fiction, but from true stories.

Vera Sováková knew that she wasn't the only one in the industry with a flexible concept of morality. Paying for news, hacking phones, firing disobedient reporters, lying in wait for politicians to make even the smallest slip – all they needed was a single wrong word. Working in the media meant all that and more. Maybe she took things a little further than most. But who knew? Vera Sováková wasn't prone to believing conspiracy theories, but sometimes big news stories and human tragedies seemed to line up surprisingly well with the economic travails of certain media companies.

Was coincidence always coincidence? Or were others moving pieces on the chessboard too?

'How do you intend to make sure your hero doesn't go rogue?' the man asked. 'That he doesn't act too soon?'

Vera knew that her hero pawn had been the biggest risk from the beginning. She had needed to manipulate his feelings and actions as precisely and subtly as possible. Vera had found the interviews, she had offered the information and she had also arranged for his house to be ransacked 'as thoroughly as possible', as she'd put it. Vera didn't even think of him as a man, but rather as a little puppet she could pull by the strings. A hero who believed he'd figured everything out alone, but who, in reality, had received each piece of information at just the moment Vera had wanted him to.

'The instructions I give him will be precise. And believe me, he has enough ambition that he'll do exactly what I say. I'll convince him that the police and rescue teams will show up in time. He wants adventure. He wants to be the face of this story. I have to hang up now. The face is here.'

Vera Sováková hung up the phone just as Jiři Hašek knocked on her door for their meeting.

23

Everything went dark. All that was before her eyes was blackness, and Lumikki liked it. For a moment, she hoped the darkness would go on and on, that she could just calmly breathe it in without thinking about anything, without even thinking about all the people around her. The stage lights came up though, revealing to the audience the shadows of a thick, dark forest where one could easily lose their way. The fairy tale could begin.

When Lenka left the café, Lumikki sat for a while in defeat. Then she set her phone on silent, because she couldn't deal with anything or anyone bothering her, and she set out into the streets.

Lenka had lied.

Lenka wasn't her sister.

The secret hadn't been revealed, and nothing had been solved. Lumikki had just been the victim of a slightly unbalanced woman's delusions. The truth was numbing. Lumikki couldn't even feel angry at Lenka. No regret. Just apathy and emptiness.

It didn't make any difference. It didn't make any difference if she never saw Lenka again. It didn't make any difference if the whole cult killed themselves. It was all the same to her. It wasn't any of her business now. She had been used as a pawn in a strange, sick mental game. She had been tricked.

Like a sleepwalker, Lumikki wandered into the old city, and on a whim, she walked through an open door that led down a set of stairs. A basement theatre where a shadow play was just starting.

She might as well spend her final days in Prague acting like a tourist and going to films and plays. That's what she came for in the first place. To discover the city alone, to be alone, to do whatever happened to feel interesting at that moment – alone. In reality, though, Lumikki knew that what she really wanted was to escape from her own thoughts and all the trauma she'd been through. Just for a moment, she wanted something different, something beautiful.

Lumikki bought a ticket and sat down in the back row on a wooden bench covered with threadbare velvet upholstery. The seats were only half full, so she had the row to herself. That was good. A girl who stank of sweat with dried blood spattered down the front of her shirt probably wasn't anyone's idea of the perfect theatre companion.

The shadow play was performed entirely without words. It wove its story for the audience using only music and shadows.

Once upon a time, there were two princesses who were the best friends in the world. They ran hand in hand through the forest, escaping beasts and monsters. They protected each other and saved each other time and time again. They combed each other's long locks and told each other stories. No one and nothing could separate them.

Lumikki watched as the shadows changed shapes and made the princesses laugh and leap over a brook to get away. They were so alive, even though they were nothing more than dark silhouettes against a light background. Lumikki emptied her mind and immersed herself in the fairy tale being told. She succeeded in shutting out Lenka, Jiři, the killer, the cult and all of Prague. She succeeded in shutting out the rest of the audience.

There were only Lumikki and the shadows.

One day, one of the princesses disappeared. The remaining princess looked and looked for her, running back and forth through the forest, weeping and wailing. But she couldn't find the other princess. A year passed, then another, and eventually, seven long years had come and gone. The sun and the moon crossed the sky thousands of times. The princess did not laugh any more. She just spent all her days sitting in the forest sadly singing a song they had once sung happily together.

Then one day, the princess learned that far, far away, beyond seven mountains and seven seas, was a tower where a princess was imprisoned. A terrible dragon guarded the tower and no one could save the princess. After hearing this, the first princess travelled past the seven mountains and seven seas to see whether this was her long-lost friend.

When she arrived at the tower, the dragon was perched upon its peak, spouting white flames that had burned all the land around completely black. The princess decided to wait patiently until the dragon fell asleep. Finally, the sky darkened and the stars appeared. The princess tried valiantly to keep her eyes open, but she fell asleep before the dragon did.

The princess awoke to someone singing the same sad song she had been singing for the past seven years. She looked up to the tower window and saw her friend. The princesses both cried for joy when they recognised each other. The princess who had arrived from afar shouted that she would save the prisoner. But the imprisoned princess replied that the time was not right because the dragon could appear at any moment and consume her with fire. Nevertheless, the princess knew that they had promised to always protect each other, and she set out to climb the tower.

When she arrived at the high window, they hugged for a long time and smiled. Suddenly, though, the look in the imprisoned princess's eyes altered. The shape of her eyes changed, and her arms changed. Her hair turned to scales, and the hem of her dress morphed into a long tail. The silk ribbons that adorned her head transformed into wings. After a moment, the princess from afar realised that she was staring into the eyes of the dragon.

However, she did not fear. Lightly touching the dragon's snout, she told her that she was still the princess inside. Or she was the princess with a dragon inside. The dragon looked at her friend and understood. Her eyes began to weep great black tears, which flowed down the walls of the tower and watered the scorched ground, making it bloom once more. The dragon princess cried, for she knew that people would not accept her because she was a dragon. And dragons would not accept her because she was a person.

Then the princess from afar wrapped her arms around the dragon's neck and promised that the two of them would stay together, come what may. They didn't need anyone else. They would look for a land where princesses and dragons could live in harmony, even if they were one and the same person.

In the final scene, the dragon flew towards the full moon with the princess on its back.

Lumikki realised her cheeks were wet. She wiped them in surprise. Had she been crying? Apparently so. She couldn't remember the last time she'd cried. She had thought she'd lost the ability to cry.

The shadow theatre story had sucked her in so thoroughly that she had forgotten herself and all her conscious thoughts. Her subconscious feelings had taken over. The story awoke images of many different things.

Lumikki and Blaze.

Lumikki and Lenka.

Lumikki and someone she played with as a child, pretending to be two girls named Snow White and Rose Red. Suddenly, she remembered the story and the game perfectly. In the story, a prince who had been turned into a bear by an enchantment helped the girls. She had loved the game even though she hadn't entirely understood it. Her playmate had been a little older than she was and told her the story as they played. Snow White and Rose Red were always together and they always saved each other, just like the princesses in the shadow play.

Lenka had saved Lumikki. No matter how much Lumikki detested her lie, she couldn't deny that Lenka had saved her.

Lenka had taken a risk and knowingly put herself in danger for Lumikki, helping her escape despite knowing that Lumikki wasn't really her sister and that helping could have meant disaster for her.

The rest of the audience had already left the theatre and the ticket seller came to the door and coughed pointedly. Lumikki stood up. She felt a little dizzy, but the feeling passed quickly when she gritted her teeth and started walking resolutely towards the door.

Lumikki hated owing people, and now she felt as though she owed Lenka her life.

Outside, the evening sun shone obliquely in Lumikki's eyes and hot air assaulted her from every side. Lumikki checked her phone. Jiři had tried to call five times. The last time was just ten minutes earlier. He'd also left a message. Lumikki tried to call him back, but when he didn't answer she listened to the message. Jiři said he was going to the White Family's house to do his story and that the mass suicide was planned for that night. The police and rescue teams were supposed to be coming to help.

Lumikki didn't stop to think. She just took off running. She could still catch Jiři at the Super8 building and go with him.

She arrived out of breath at 6:15 p.m. The receptionist looked her over from head to toe with pity in her eyes.

'Hard day?'

'And it might get worse. Is Jiři still here?'

'No. He just left. He didn't say where but –'

Just then, a woman of about forty stepped out of the lift

and did a double take when she saw Lumikki. It was as if the woman recognised her, though Lumikki couldn't remember ever having seen her before. There was something in her gaze that was so frightening Lumikki felt the hair on the back of her neck stand up. The woman sped up, lifting her phone to her ear and taking one more sharp glance at Lumikki before stepping outside.

'Who was that?' Lumikki asked the receptionist, who looked at her wide-eyed.

'You don't know? That's Vera Sováková, Super8's CEO.

Lumikki just waved her hand in thanks and ran out the door.

She had to get to Lenka's house before this tragedy could become real.

24

The first thing Jiři noticed was the smell, which was acrid and nearly suffocating. For a moment, he couldn't place it, until it triggered a memory from a summer he had spent at youth camp ten years earlier. They'd spent every night sitting around a fire. Because the summer was rainy, it was impossible to get the damp wood to light with just matches and newspaper. They went through lighter fluid by the gallon.

Someone was using lighter fluid here too. But more. Dozens, maybe even hundreds of gallons. Jiři had to be careful not to trip on the bundles of fabric strewn on the floor. They were all soaked through.

There was no one around. There was no sound.

Jiři didn't think that was a good sign. In fact, it was a very bad sign. He didn't believe for a second that the cult members had left or decided to abandon their plan. No one would waste this much time, energy and lighter fluid just to burn down a dilapidated house. They were definitely still in the building. Somewhere deep inside.

The ground floor seemed to be empty. The doors connecting the rooms were open. The pieces of fabric doused in lighter fluid were scattered everywhere, on the floors and draped over the sparse furnishings. One good spark would set the whole place ablaze instantly. That was obviously the point.

He lifted his camera and panned over the first floor, keeping his hand as steady as he could, and then set off up the stairs. It was still as quiet as the grave. Jiři desperately hoped he hadn't come too late.

Lenka thought of her mother.

Her mother's hands as she stroked and braided her hair. Their softness and power. Their strength, always there, determined but never heavy-handed. Her mother's hands had been adept and nimble. They could just as easily form a perfectly curved croissant as clear a clogged drain or fix a door with a broken hinge.

Her mother's hair, which tickled her face when her mother bent down to give her a goodnight kiss. Mother had insisted on doing this even when Lenka thought she was too old for goodnight kisses. As a teenager, she had protested and pulled the covers over her head, hiding under them. Mother had patiently kissed her through the covers so that Lenka only felt it as a soft pressure. At some point, Lenka had started willingly offering her cheek or forehead or hair for a kiss again, secretly happy that her mother had turned a deaf ear to her objections.

Lenka knew she wasn't supposed to think about her mother. She was supposed to think about Jesus. She was supposed to think about the paradise they were about to travel to. The home where their family could finally be in direct communion with

195

God. Mother didn't belong to the family any more. Mother had betrayed the family.

Lenka could tell from her wooziness that the sleeping pills were starting to take effect. Soon, she would slip over the edge into unconsciousness. She wouldn't smell the stench of the lighter fluid emanating from her white dress. She wouldn't hear the murmured prayers of the people lying around her any more. Soon, they too would fall silent as they slept. Lenka didn't pray. She didn't need to. She believed that faith was enough to carry her past the dark emotion of fear. She only hoped that, when the flames began to lick her skin, she would already be so asleep that she wouldn't even realise. No pain, not even distantly felt through layers of sleep.

Mother. Lenka's thoughts stubbornly returned to her mother. Maybe it wasn't unreasonable to think that she might see her again after she died. Lenka wanted to believe in a kind of mercy and forgiveness that transcended what the family had taught her. She didn't want to imagine a God who would cast aside her mother for her mistakes. Lenka's God wouldn't do that. The family didn't know. They thought God was hard, merciless and demanding, admitting into his presence only a select few. The chosen ones. Life in death.

That's what the family said. That in death they would find their new, real life.

Lenka couldn't feel her feet any more. She couldn't feel her hands. Her body had already fallen asleep, but her mind still hovered on the edge.

Life.

Had this been her life, like this, as a mortal? Nothing more than this? She had never visited any other countries. She had never kissed anyone. She had never stayed up all night talking to a friend. She had never been so furious that all she wanted to do was scream and cry. She had never been drunk. She had never been lost in a strange city. She had never laughed so hard she couldn't breathe.

Sleep dragged Lenka down even as her conscious mind seized in panic at one last thought: *I don't want to die yet. I want to live.*

I want to live.

I want . . .

Lumikki hauled herself up onto the high iron fence. Her legs were shaking with fatigue, and her hands were so sweaty she could barely grip the bars. Now wasn't the time to worry, though. Now she had to get into the house as fast as possible.

The spikes that topped the fence were sharp. Lumikki tried to grip them as high as she could, so she could swing herself over in one fluid motion. However, one hand slipped at the key moment and she felt a spike dig a long scrape into her thigh, which immediately began oozing blood. The pain made her balance fail, and she crashed into the yard on her side, not on her feet as she'd intended. Fortunately, she had the presence of mind to pull her elbows close into her body and tuck her chin into her chest to guard her neck.

Lumikki rolled a couple of times after the fall and, once she'd come to rest, lay still for a few seconds to catch her breath. Her ribs hurt and the scrape on her leg stung, but otherwise she was fine. No broken bones or serious bruises. She had experienced much worse in her life. She had limped home from school far more battered than this and pretended nothing had happened.

Lumikki stood up. Her legs were weak, and she felt a little light-headed, but she could still walk. Dehydration was probably making her feel worse than any other single factor.

No one was in the yard. Lumikki might make it in time.

She wasn't sure, but after seeing Vera Sováková, the strongest impression had come over her that this woman knew more about the suicide plan than anyone else. She might even be involved in it somehow. Because who was going to benefit from the plan? Of course Adam Havel/Smith, who would flee the cult because he had already pumped as much money out of them as he could and they were only a burden now. But also the media, which would feast on every last morsel of tragedy. It was Super8 that had an up-and-coming reporter investigating the cult. And it was that reporter's boss who had sent him alone to cover a dangerous story. Wasn't it a little too convenient that information about the exact timing of the suicide had come first to Super8?

Lumikki ran to the side door and found it already broken open. At the door, she caught a familiar scent. Jiři's aftershave. That meant that Jiři was here too but hadn't been for long. The thought gave Lumikki more confidence. They could do this together. *Unless* . . .

That one nagging word. In Lumikki's mind, it expanded into a full sentence. Unless Jiři was involved in the plot? It was perfectly possible. In fact, it was probable. What sense would there be in sending a man to do a job who didn't know what was going on behind the scenes?

And if that was true, Lumikki didn't know who she should be most afraid of meeting in the house. There wasn't time to think. There wasn't time to analyse. Lumikki stepped through the door into the overwhelming stench of lighter fluid.

25

Vera Sováková took a few deep breaths and savoured the moment. Now it would begin. She had been patiently preparing this media spectacle for a long time now. Adam Havel had approached her years earlier, offering an exclusive on the White Family – for a price, of course. Vera thought the story needed something more, though. Together they began planning a tragedy large enough to capture the attention of the whole country.

Vera imagined people falling silent one after another in the cafés and bistros of Prague. Someone tried to continue chatting, but he was shushed instantly. In homes, people watched in amazement as the live news broadcast interrupted their quiz show. Mobile phones rang. 'Turn on the TV. Something's happening.'

The screen, which displayed the Super8 logo in the bottom corner, was suddenly full of hand-camera footage of an old, rundown house. A matter-of-fact female voice, which some, to their surprise, recognised as the head of Super8, longtime reporter turned chief executive Vera Sováková, related that one of their journalists, Jiři Hašek, had just gained entrance to the house of a dangerous cult, the White Family. His sources told him that the cult was planning a mass suicide, and it was set to happen at any moment. Jiří Hašek had been first on the scene and gallantly, braving death, had entered the house in hope of saving the victims.

Vera felt shivers up her spine imagining all the people glued to their television sets. They would just now be realising that they were watching a true-life drama unfold before their eyes. An unscripted drama that could end in triumph or devastation.

A single match would have been enough. Adam Havel wasn't going to take any risks, though. He hefted the heavy Molotov cocktail in his hand and hurled it at the window. The glass shattered and the room burst into flames.

Idiots. They believed Adam when he said he'd make sure they were all in a deep sleep before lighting the fire for them all – himself included. He had fulfilled the first part of that promise. He did watch to make sure everyone was asleep. Then he locked the door and went outside. He waited until he saw the stupid reporter break in through the side door.

Adam Havel would have preferred to stay and watch as the ugly old house went up like a torch. As it devoured these people's stupidity and credulity. He felt a sort of satisfaction at being able to complete here what he had bungled in Nebraska. This time, he had built his community more patiently, until each and every member trusted him implicitly. Until his stories about cleansing fire lifting their souls directly to a heaven that unbelievers could not attain were the truest things in their lives.

201

Adam had enjoyed the power he had over them. From time to time, he had even toyed with the idea of letting everything continue as it was. Adam had talked about faith and family so convincingly that sometimes he even started to believe it himself. But shepherding his flock had become increasingly tedious, and he was getting old. The deal with Vera Sováková gave him a way to leave free and rich.

Adam couldn't stay to watch the conflagration he had started. His flight was leaving soon to carry him far away from here, with the money from Vera and a brand new name and passport. It was time to start over with a clean slate. Clean and white as snow.

Adam Havel turned his back on the house and locked the large iron gate behind him. That would slow down the police and fire department for a few seconds. Probably the crucial seconds.

Shards of glass came flying at Lumikki and she dropped into a protective crouch. Then the heat from the bundles of fabric bursting into flames hit her. Lumikki dashed to the stairs. On the upper landing, she collided with Jiři and his camera.

'What are you doing?' Lumikki hissed and put her hand over the lens.

Jiři jerked the camera back.

'I'm filming.'

Lumikki swallowed. Her muscles were tense.

'Are you part of this plot?'

'What do you mean?'

Jiři's voice and eyes were sincerely confused. But if Lumikki had learned one thing on this hellish trip, it was that she wasn't as good at spotting a lie as she thought.

There wasn't time for subtlety now. They needed all their cards on the table.

'Vera gave me instructions to –' Jiři began.

'I think Vera Sováková is partially behind this. I think she's known for a long time what was going to happen. She was probably the one who sent the hit man after me. This whole mass suicide might even be her handiwork.'

Lumikki spoke quickly in hushed tones. Hot dark-grey smoke rose from the ground floor and flames crackled. They both started coughing. Lumikki could see Jiři weighing her words. He was going through each and every event and piece of information that had led them to this moment. Then his eyes went wide. He had clearly decided that Lumikki might be right. He shut off the camera.

'They aren't on the second or third floors. They must be in the basement,' Jiři said.

Lumikki started down the stairs.

'Wait! It isn't safe here. You need to get out now. The fire department will be here soon. They were tipped off in advance,' Jiři said. 'Vera said that . . .'

Jiři trailed off when he understood.

'They weren't tipped off about anything,' Lumikki replied. 'I called the emergency line just to be sure. No one had heard anything about a mass suicide. I don't know if they believed me. They probably thought I was insane. I didn't have time to wait around trying to convince them. They might be getting another call right now from one of the neighbours.'

'I'll call,' Jiři said, and started pulling out his phone.

The fire climbed the walls to the upper floors. Rags soaked in lighter fluid weren't enough any more. Now it was hungry for wood. The temperature was getting unbearable. The fire sank its burning teeth into the top of the stairs and the wood began to give way.

'No time!' Lumikki yelled.

They pounded down the stairs.

Jiři tossed the camera aside. Nothing unnecessary.

'Follow me!' Lumikki yelled and started weaving along the only path that wasn't yet a sea of flames.

She heard the sound of fabric ripping behind her. Jiři was tearing strips from his shirt. He handed one to Lumikki.

'Here! Put it over your mouth.'

They arrived at the stairs to the basement. Going underground felt like pure insanity with a house built entirely from wood blazing around them. There wasn't time to think about what was crazy and what wasn't now though. Just then, the sound of something large collapsing came from behind them. Probably the upper flight of stairs. They rushed down into the basement.

Storage rooms. A food pantry. And one room with a locked door. Jiři and Lumikki looked at each other, nodded and then kicked the door as hard as they could. The wood gave way a little, but not enough. They kicked again. The door complained, but held.

The temperature of the air around them was climbing alarmingly fast. A fiery furnace. A lake of fire. Hell.

Lumikki's eyes were watering. As if through a veil, she saw Jiři crouch down and run into a storage room. After what felt like an eternity, he returned carrying a heavy chainsaw.

Jiři jerked the starter rope several times, but the chainsaw didn't make a sound. Lumikki could tell that he had never started a chainsaw before. Lumikki had used them more times than she could remember – at her cousins' summer house in Åland. She rushed over to Jiři and bodily pushed him away from the saw. There was a time and a place for politeness, and this wasn't it.

Lumikki wished the saw had been recently used, because then starting it would have been easy. She held the saw against the ground by placing her left foot halfway through the rear handle and holding the front handle tightly in her left hand. With her right hand, she made a few short pulls on the starter rope and then one good, long pull to finish.

Nothing.

Start already. Start.

Lumikki tried again. Three short pulls to draw fuel mixture into the cylinder. Then one long, fast pull.

The chainsaw growled into life.

It was heavy, but Lumikki managed to lift it up into the right position. Her arm muscles trembled with the effort when the blade dug into the door. Lumikki turned her face away as slivers and sawdust began flying. The noise was deafening. She succeeded in cutting a large gash in the door before her strength gave out.

'Move!' Jiři yelled behind her.

As Lumikki got out of the way, Jiři took a few running steps and kicked the spot she had cut. The door split down the middle.

People lay on the floor of the room. Lumikki quickly counted seventeen. They looked dead, but when Lumikki touched the neck of an old woman lying nearby she felt a pulse.

'They've been drugged!' she screamed.

The fire was crackling so loudly above them that it was hard to hear.

'Adam Havel isn't here,' Jiři called back.

'It doesn't matter. Help me save Lenka!'

Lumikki had found her among the others. She tried to lift her up, but Lenka's body was limp and heavy. Jiři came to help, and together they got her into Jiři's arms. Lumikki also swung Lenka's arm over her own neck to take some of the weight.

Slowly and carefully, they started climbing the narrow stairs. Stinging smoke assailed their eyes and noses and lungs. The heat slammed into them.

The ground floor was an inferno, but they could still see the side door. Slipping out from under Lenka's arm, Lumikki tapped Jiři on the back and screamed over the blaze.

'Run!'

Jiři took off. Lumikki followed right behind. Suddenly, a burning board fell from the ceiling. Lumikki just managed to jump backwards. She watched through the smoke as Jiři made it to the side door and out to safety with Lenka in his arms.

The fire shrieked and sang around Lumikki. She felt it licking her shirt and thought her back was on fire.

Closing her eyes against the smoke, Lumikki just ran and ran and ran through the fire, out the door and threw herself on the grass, rolling and rolling and rolling and rolling until the burning on her back disappeared. She saw Jiři lying on the grass, coughing. She saw Lenka, who lay next to him in a deep, peaceful sleep.

The flames licked at the sky.

And over the roar of the fire came the sound of fire engines in the distance.

THURSDAY, 23 JUNE

EPILOGUE

We are difficult to understand
It was hard to make this simple plan work
Difficult, but that's what made it burn

Lumikki looked at the white cotton balls, whipped-cream mountains and blue depths through the window of the aeroplane as she let Shirley Manson sing in her ears about a big, bright, shining world. The song was uncommonly sunny for Garbage, but right now Lumikki liked that.

She let her thoughts rest on the view outside. Rest. That's what she needed now more than anything. She wanted to lock herself in her apartment and sleep for a week. That wasn't an option, though. Her family's midsummer get-together was coming up. She would have to tell everyone what Prague had been like.

Lovely.
Very Central European.
Lots of culture. I even went to a shadow play.
Relaxing.

And she could talk about the city's hills and parks, all the bridges, the heat during the day that turned to a caressing warmth at night, the alleys of the old city, the statues, the cafés. She could tell them about all the good, easy things. And when they asked if she ever wanted to go back to Prague, she could answer honestly yes, she'd go back any time. What she would leave out was the two friends she had waiting there. She had spent the last days of her trip with Jiři and Lenka. Apparently, Vera Sováková had called the hit man off after the mass suicide attempt was over. Lumikki wasn't a threat any more. She wasn't significant. And for that, Lumikki was extremely grateful.

But she knew that all anyone would want to hear about was the fire and the rescue. The entire local media had wanted to interview the 'miracle girl' who had happened along and helped save people when the White Family cult was trying to commit suicide. Even though Lumikki had said as little as possible during the interviews and tried to direct the reporters to Jiři, she was the one they were interested in. All the reporters thought Lumikki was just the kind of sympathetic yet vulnerable hero the viewing audience loved. They showed clips of her on all the news reports with her soot-smeared face and blackened clothes.

Even now, she could see the man sitting on the other side of the aisle in the aeroplane reading a magazine with her picture on the cover. Her short hair was mussed, her eyes looked red and weepy because of the smoke and on her left cheek was a scratch left by a splinter of wood from the door. Lumikki knew that, inside, there was also a picture of the chainsaw and a description of how a 'brave Finnish girl raised surrounded by forests' had broken through the door.

When the businessman lifted his eyes, Lumikki turned to look out of the window again. Maybe no one would recognise her with a clean face and clothes. Still, she didn't want to risk having to rehash the events surrounding the fire one more time for a complete stranger.

Her mum and dad and relatives were going to interrogate her, though, no matter how much Lumikki would prefer to forget. The news coverage of the staged tragedy revolted her, even though a much greater tragedy had been averted.

So there you had it. Vera Sováková had got her headlines, but smaller ones than she'd planned. Not enough death, not big enough news. Only death can make a true legend. The firemen arrived on the scene too early. A bunch of minor injuries wasn't nearly as thrilling as an entire cult dying a fiery death – one old lady with third-degree burns was the only real victim.

They didn't catch Adam Havel. The police issued a warrant for his arrest, but Jiři suspected no one would ever find him. Adam Smith had also been a made-up name. There was no information about his real identity. He could be anywhere in the world. Maybe gathering a new group of needy people around him.

Of course, there was no evidence of Vera Sováková's role in the events. When Jiři tried to twist her arm a little, she just observed what a long line of applicants there was to become a reporter at Super8. Jiři told Lumikki that maybe one day soon he would tell Vera Sováková to go ahead and pick someone from that line to replace him. But not quite yet. Now he had another person to take care of, and that took money.

When you save someone, you become responsible for them. That's what Jiři had said when he invited Lenka to live with him. At least for a while. Until she could get her life started again.

At the airport, Lenka had hugged Lumikki long and hard.

'If I did have a sister . . .' Lenka had begun.

Lumikki had smiled and nodded.

Inside this big, bright world
Inside this big, bright world
Inside this big, bright world

Now Lumikki looked at the brightness of the sun and the whiteness of the clouds and thought that even though the trip hadn't brought an answer to the mysteries of her past, it had provided hints. Lumikki was surer than ever that Lenka had landed surprisingly close to the truth with her concocted story about them being sisters. The dreams and memories that Lenka's lie had awoken were true. Lumikki knew that she hadn't imagined the Snow White and Rose Red game or any of the rest of it. It had all happened.

Once upon a time, she had a sister.

Thank you for choosing a Hot Key book.

If you want to know more about our authors and what we publish, you can find us online.

You can start at our website

www.hotkeybooks.com

And you can also find us on:

We hope to see you soon!